DIARY OF A 5TH GRADE
OUTLAW
WHO IS THE BUCKS BANDIT?

epic! originals

DIARY OF A 5TH GRADE
OUTLAW

WHO IS THE BUCKS BANDIT?

GINA LOVELESS

ILLUSTRATIONS BY
ANDREA BELL

Andrews McMeel
PUBLISHING®

DIARY OF A 5TH GRADE OUTLAW:
WHO IS THE BUCKS BANDIT?

Andrews Mcmeel Publishing
a division of Andrews Mcmeel Universal
1130 Walnut Street, Kansas City, Missouri 64106

www.andrewsmcmeel.com

Epic! Creations, Inc.
702 Marshall Street, Suite 280, Redwood City, California 94063

www.getepic.com

20 21 22 23 24 SDB 10 9 8 7 6 5 4 3 2 1

ISBN: 978-1-5248-6089-9

Library of Congress Control Number: 2020930103

Design by Dan Nordskog

Made by:
King Yip (Dongguan) Printing & Packaging Factory Ltd.
Address and location of production:
Daning Administrative District, Humen Town
Dongguan Guangdong, China 523930
1st Printing—6/1/20

TO MOM AND DAD, FOR TEACHING ME THE RIGHT TIMES TO TRUST MY GUT.

BEST PART OF HALLOWEEN?

SCARY STORIES?

COSTUMES?

CANDY?

MONDAY, OCTOBER 31

If anyone out there is reading my journal, I bet they think I love Halloween for one reason: Halloween candy.

For the last month, I've probably

written about food at least a hundred times in this journal, so I could see why they'd think that.

And sure, candy is great.

But I'm not really into Halloween. For one thing, I don't have my friend Mary Ann to trick-or-treat with because her family goes on vacation around then. Also, Halloween stories can be *really* scary. Like, with zombies and vampires being *real*. That's too much scariness for me.

Plus, kids at my school and in my neighborhood go all-out, with fancy face paint and handmade costumes that look like they cost a thousand bucks. My mom and dad would totally get me a cool costume if we could afford it, but we don't have money for that sort of stuff.

But this year, I might change my mind about Halloween. That's because Mary Ann is actually here this week. And on top of that, I have a really simple costume that is so cool it's crazy.

A few days ago, Ms. Gaffey, my teacher, read us a really, really, *really* old story about this guy named Robin Hood. And it turns out that I have all kinds of stuff in common with him!

Dude-Robin had a bunch of

friends called Merry Men. My friends call each other the Merry Misfits because we're a pretty happy group, and we're also a bunch of weirdos, in a good way.

Dude-Robin used to steal from the rich and give to the poor with his best buddy, Little John. A few weeks ago, my new friend LJ and I basically did the same thing when my former enemy, Nadia, was getting rich by making kids hand over Bonus Bucks—our school's way of rewarding students. LJ and I ended up stealing all of the Bonus Bucks from Nadia and returning them to every kid in the school.

Learning about Robin Hood gave me a great idea for the perfect costume!

At first, I was worried about how I'd include the bow and arrow he carried around. I knew Principal Roberta wouldn't let me into the school with something so dangerous. But I had a way around that.

When I walked into the classroom this morning, I looked around for my friends, but none of them were there yet. So I walked over to my desk and unpacked my backpack.

But then I heard a bunch of oohs and aahs from the other kids in the class, and I turned around to see what was going on.

There were my friends in their costumes, and I think I smiled as big as a pancake when I saw all of them.

Mmmmm. I should really ask Dad to make pancakes on Sunday.

"You guys look awesome," I said.

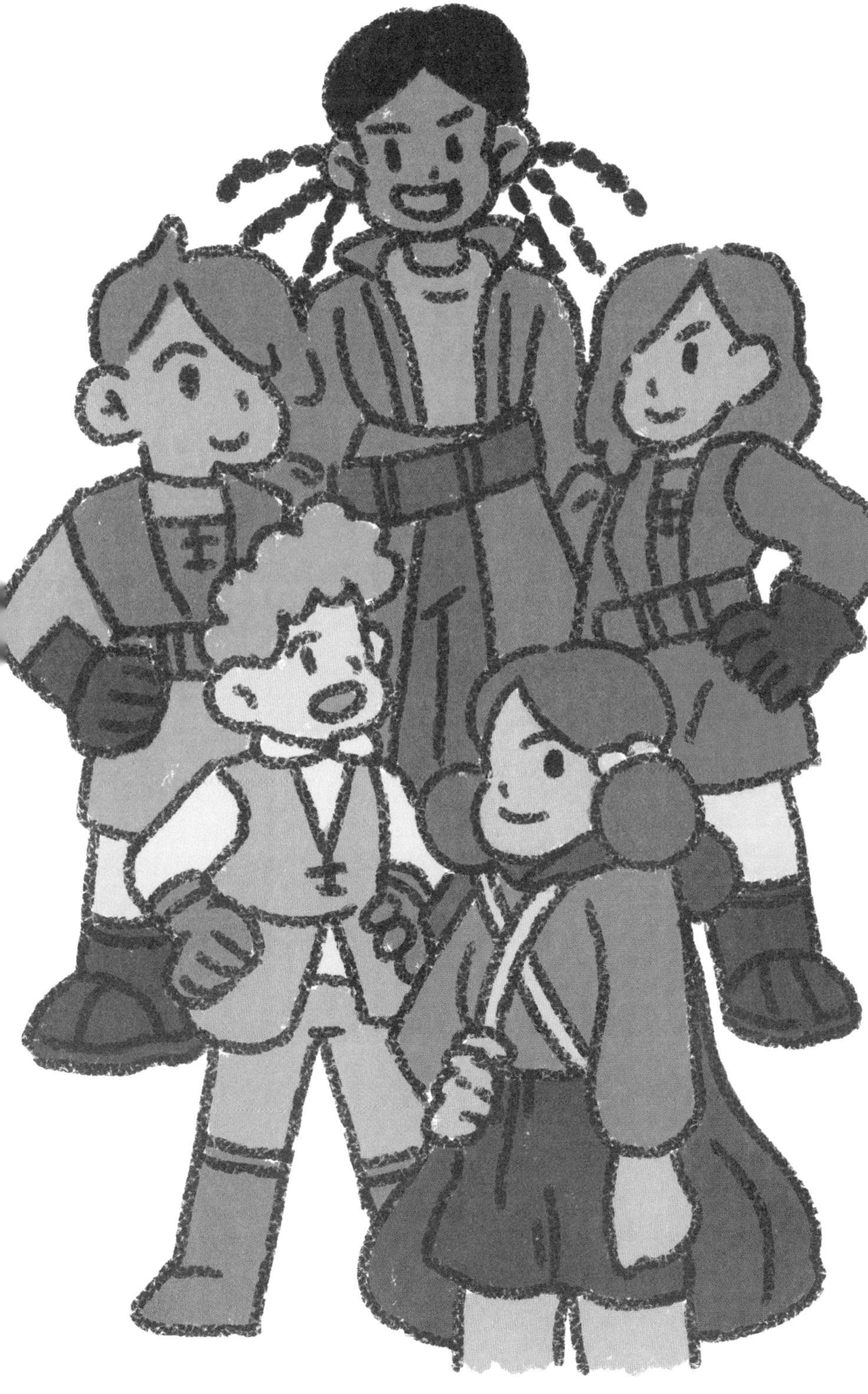

Nadia tugged on her belt and said, "Even me?"

I looked at her like she had purple gummy worms stuck to her face. "I'm not sure who you're supposed to be," I said.

Nadia gave me a big smile. "I'm the Sheriff of Nottingham in that Robin Hood story. He was Robin's enemy! It was too perfect!"

I laughed and shook my head. Nadia and I used to clash a lot because she used to be a big bully. When all of my friends tried to convince me that she wasn't too bad, I didn't believe them, and it didn't go so well for me. Now we're okay with each other, and we aren't enemies anymore, but she was right—it was the perfect costume for her.

Allana and Dale looked at each other and nodded. That meant they were about to start one of their signature raps. Dale started this one.

It's Halloween
    At school today
And we are so
    Ready to play.
With scary stories
    In the library
That will make us
    Want to flee!

Plus scary movies
With all the grades
While we sip on
Our limeades.
And we know Ms. Gaffey
Has fun in store
With spooky projects
That won't be a bore.

The twins stopped rapping and looked around. I think they were making sure Ms. Gaffey wasn't in the room yet.

The coast was clear, so they finished the rest of the rap while walking to their desks.

Let's start today

With a little gloom

With a scary rap

About a scary bathroom

When you walk inside

You would think

It's totally normal

Until you try the sink…

Turn the handles

And you will see

Something RED pouring out

That's warm and sticky

Even if it's not

What you think

It'll make you run

Like water out of a sink!

Then they clapped their hands together and let out an evil laugh that sounded like "Mwuhahahaha" as they walked back to their seats.

The classroom freaked out. Applause echoed off the ceiling and I swear we all screamed and hollered so loud that I wondered if I'd be able to hear anything for the rest of the day.

It was an "Ahem" that came from the door that made everyone stop making noise. We all ran to our seats and turned to the front of the classroom with our biggest puppy dog eyes.

There stood Ms. Gaffey, dressed like a hot dog, next to a boy who didn't look like he was dressed for Halloween at all.

MYSTERY KID

rose → behind ear

longish ↗ black hair

striped ↗ shirt

And just like that, I was hungry for hot dogs.

Note to self: Ask Dad to grill up hot dogs sometime soon.

From a few seats over, Sammy whispered, "Who's that kid?"

LJ, who sat behind me, said, "No idea. Who do you think he's supposed to be?"

I looked at him like he was holding a piece of pizza upside down—which is a little odd (but not as odd as liking pizza at all!)

"Maybe nobody?" I said. "Maybe he didn't know you could dress up on Halloween?"

"So...he just wears a rose

14

behind his ear on regular days?"
Allana asked.

She had a good point. This kid
seemed pretty off.

Okay, that sounds really bad.
Let me be clear: it wasn't because of
the way he looked. I wear a hoodie
every single day, no matter how hot
it is outside. I once wore my hoodie
on a day so hot I had sweat stains
in my armpits that looked like I
had just squirted full juice boxes
into them.

But there was something about
him I couldn't quite explain.

Then again, I had no idea if I
should be trying to explain it.

Last week, when I had a bad feeling about Nadia, and I thought she was trying to trick all of my friends into some big nasty scheme of hers, I was totally wrong. It turned out *I'd* been the nasty one.

I didn't even know this kid's name yet, and I was sitting there, looking at him, thinking that he seemed like he was up to no good or something.

But I've learned that I need to give people a chance.

Then again, I still had this feeling pushing up through my stomach.

And I was 99.99999 percent sure it wasn't a hungry feeling.

Although, come to think of it, I was also pretty hungry.

Why did Ms. Gaffey have to dress up as a hot dog this year?

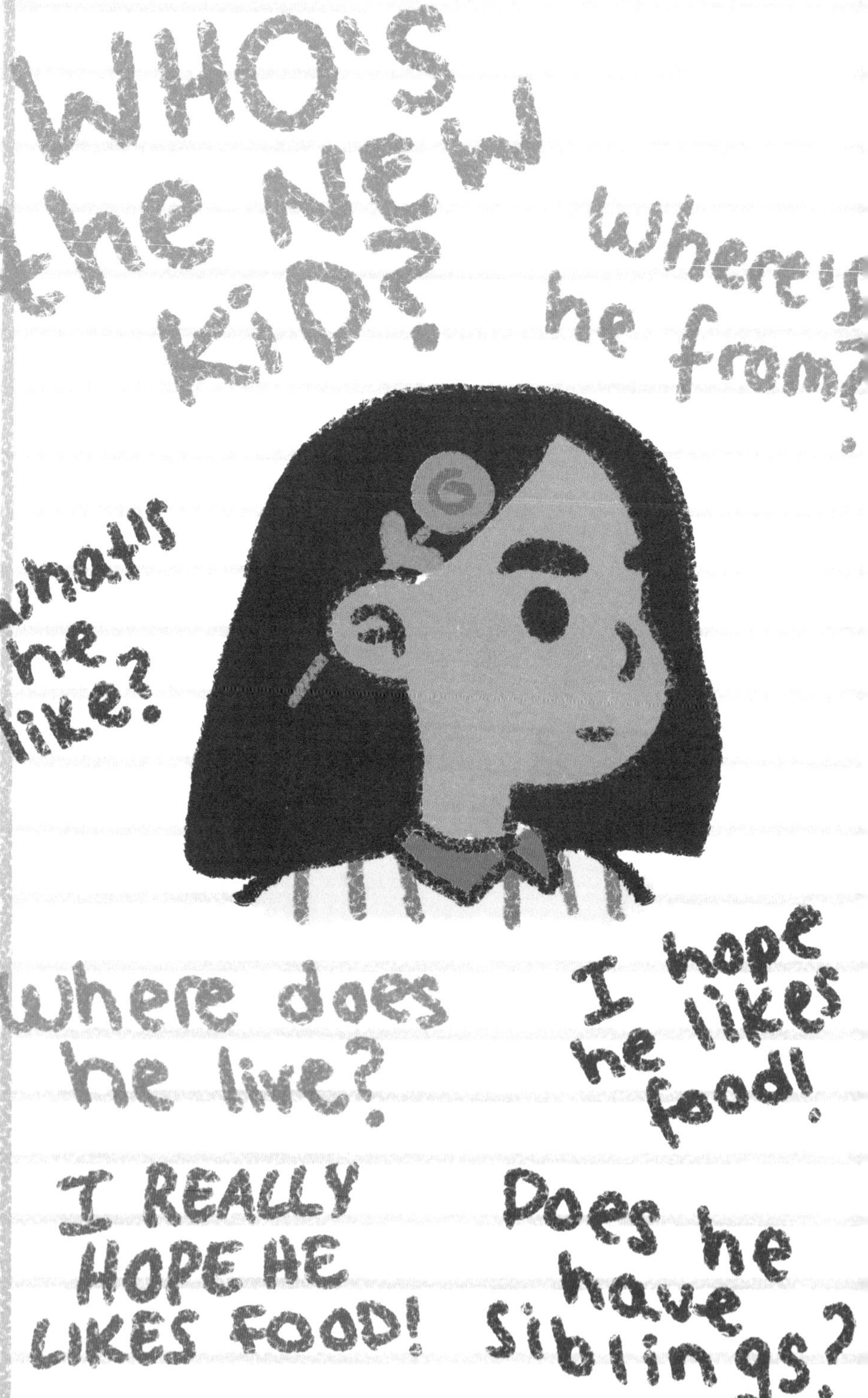

WHO'S the NEW KiD?
Where's he from?
what's he like?
Where does he live?
I hope he likes food!
I REALLY HOPE HE LIKES FOOD!
Does he have siblings?

CHAPTER 2

Everyone whispered about the mystery boy until Ms. Gaffey cleared her throat.

"Let's all welcome Wilu Johnson to our class. He joins us after living in Texas. Is that right, Wilu?"

"I'm originally from California,

but then we moved to Colorado, and then Texas."

Then Ms. Gaffey wrote the new kid's name twice on the board.

"The top is how you spell Wilu's name, and the bottom is how you pronounce it." Then she sat down and looked at Wilu. "Would you like to tell the class a little about yourself?"

"Sure," he said. "I've moved a lot because of my mom. She works in sales and moves around to train people to be as good at it as she is. My dad stays at home with my little brother."

"And what about you, Wilu?" Ms. Gaffey asked. "What do you like to do for fun?"

He scrunched up his face and looked at the ceiling. "I'm a big sports fan. And I guess that's all I'd like to say."

The weird feeling popped up in my stomach again, but I tried to push it down. Why did Wilu seem polite, but also a little bit rude at the same time? I didn't have answers yet, so I just kept listening to see if I'd be able to figure out more about this mystery kid.

"All right then," Ms. Gaffey said. "Class, any questions for Wilu?"

Josh Blues raised his hand and Ms. Gaffey pointed to him. "Yeah, what's your favorite team?" he asked.

Wilu scrunched up his face and looked at the ceiling again. "Well, I really like the North Carolina Courage, but the Orlando Pride is a close second."

Josh looked at Wilu like Wilu was an avocado, and Josh didn't actually know what an avocado was. After a long pause, Josh said, "Those aren't sports teams."

I love basketball, but I couldn't remember ever hearing of those teams either. Maybe they were hockey teams?

LJ is into a lot of different sports. She said, "Do you mean the North Carolina Tar Heels? That's college basketball."

Sammy loves football, so I wasn't surprised at all when he said, "Maybe he meant the Miami Dolphins."

But Wilu crossed his arms. "I didn't mean any of those. I'm into women's professional soccer teams." He pulled a wallet out of his pocket and held out a picture:

"That's me and two of the starting forwards," he said as he walked up and down the rows of desks.

Everyone giggled.

Well, everyone except LJ, Sammy, Allana, Dale, and me.

Wilu didn't seem bothered by the laughter. "My mother taught me that anyone can play any sport they want and anyone can like any sport they want."

That made the feeling in my stomach go away a bit. I liked that he wasn't afraid to stick up for himself.

Tara Hutter raised her hand, put

it back down, and started asking her question before Ms. Gaffey even called on her.

"What's your costume supposed to be?" she asked.

"I'm meeting someone."

I'd thought Josh had given Wilu a confused look, but Tara's look was ten times more baffled. "Huh?" she said. "That's not a costume."

"Yes, it is," he said. "My mother met my father in a bookstore. They both carried a single rose so they would recognize each other. So, that's what I am for Halloween. I'm meeting someone."

Ms. Gaffey stood up and said,

"All right everyone, let's be warm to Wilu and give him a chance to settle into our classroom."

She pulled something out of her desk that was hard to see, at first. But when she lifted it up, I realized it was the coolest thing she could possibly give him.

"Here are five Bonus Bucks, to start you off," she said.

Now it was Wilu's turn to look at Ms. Gaffey like she had carrots in her hand and he had no idea why she'd give him carrots at a time like this.

"Thank you, but what are they?" he asked.

"They're a reward system here at our school. You earn them for doing well on tests or being helpful to others."

I was sure Wilu would be excited now that Ms. Gaffey had explained what they were. I was sure he would say, "Wow. That sounds awesome. Could you tell me about what I might buy with them?"

But . . . yeah. He didn't do anything like that.

Instead, Wilu shrugged, took the bucks, and sat in an empty seat near Sammy.

I've never been more confused about a kid before. There were things I thought were pretty cool about him, like that he knew what he liked and he didn't care what other kids thought.

I especially liked that he didn't care what Josh Blues thought. Josh once told me I was weird because I liked fish sticks, which is bananas, because who doesn't love something crispy on the outside and flaky on the inside?

Just when I thought I was starting to figure Wilu out, LJ tapped me on the shoulder and said, "That's a misfit if I ever saw one."

I nodded. "We should ask him to sit with us at lunch," I said.

LJ gave me a thumbs-up. Then she leaned across the aisle and whispered to Allana, who gave us both a thumbs-up. Allana whispered to Dale, who nodded his head. And then Dale whispered to Sammy, who smiled wide.

Sammy turned to Wilu. I was pretty sure Sammy said something like, "My friends and I wanted to know if you'd like to sit with us at lunch today."

I was sure Sammy would give us a big thumbs-up and Wilu would join us at lunch.

But yeah ... it didn't go like that at all.

Wilu didn't want to sit with us at lunch. I was trying to keep an open mind, but I also couldn't help but think, *What on earth is up with this new kid?*

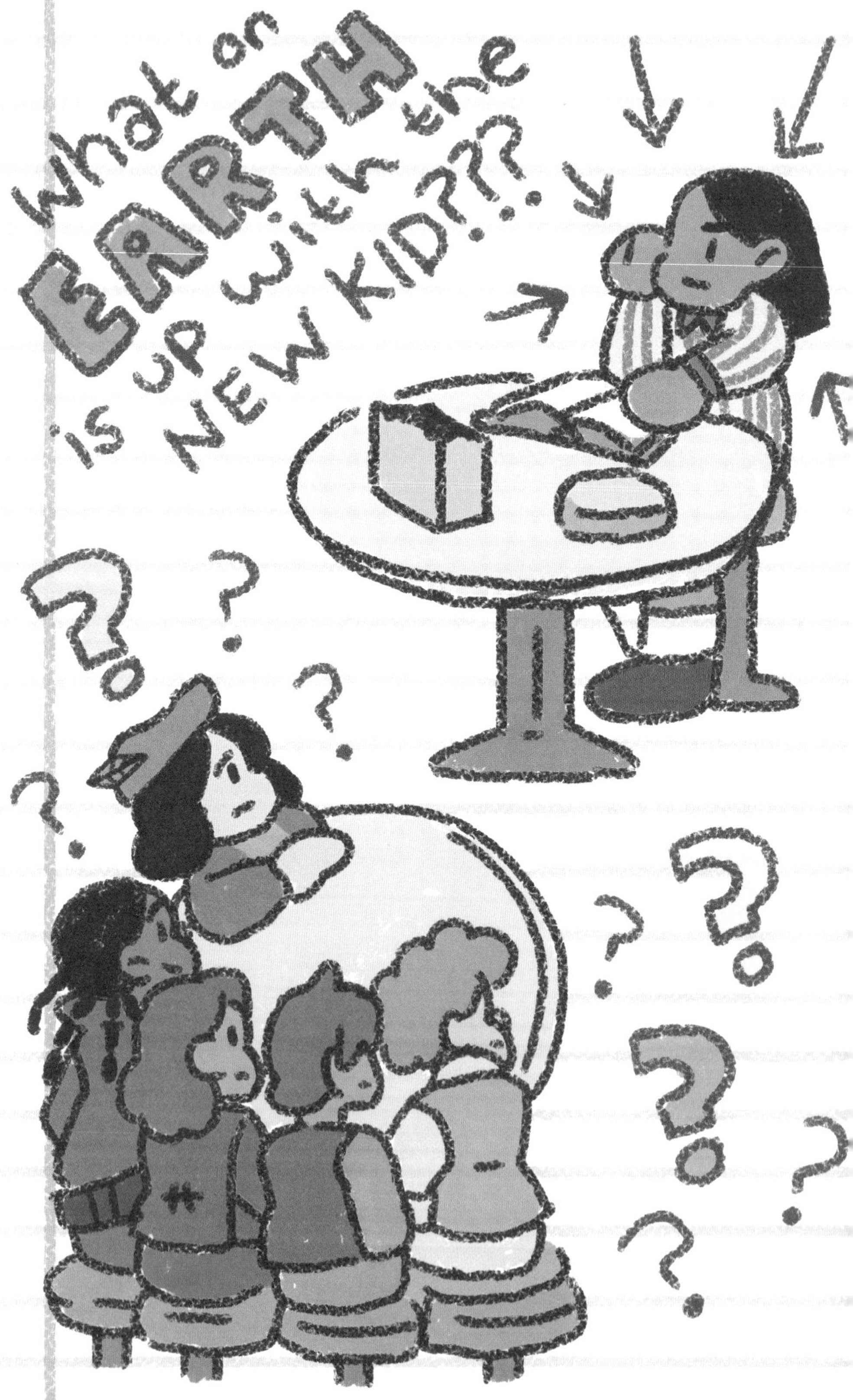
What on EARTH is up with the NEW KID???

CHAPTER 3

I think Ms. Gaffey knew we'd be thinking about all the cool stuff Principal Roberta had planned for the afternoon, so she planned some fun, spooky activities for the morning, too. Here are just a few of the things that we did:

We stuck our hands in bags and had to guess what the stuff inside really was.

EYES

intestines

We made homemade slime. Well... some of us did.

But the best was making ghosts fly in the air. Because of science!

It was so much fun, I had almost completely forgotten about the new kid.

Plus, I was so ready for lunch. Staring at Ms. Gaffey as a hot dog all morning had made my stomach do backflips.

Everyone grabbed their lunches and headed to the cafeteria. Sammy, Allana, and Dale all sat down while LJ and I grabbed a few extra chairs. We had a pretty big group of friends sitting together now.

Nadia came over and plopped down next to LJ.

"Did you see? New kid is sitting by himself," she said.

We all looked over to where Nadia pointed. Wilu sat alone, reading a book and eating his lunch out of a brown paper bag.

Sammy looked back first. "Maybe he really is meeting someone?"

"Who could he be meeting?" Nadia asked. "It's his first day."

"I think his costume was supposed to be funny," I said.

"I think it's strange," Nadia said.

I thought I'd say something like, "I know, me too." I thought I'd tell everyone I had a funny feeling about Wilu.

But it turns out, I couldn't even see my own reactions coming.

"That doesn't mean it's not funny," I said.

I thought about what I'd said for a second. Why did I defend Wilu?

Was it because I feel bad for him? I certainly don't understand Wilu, but I also don't think people should tease him just because they don't understand him.

Maybe it was simpler than that. Maybe I just don't like Nadia saying mean things. Maybe I felt like her bully side was sticking around, and I didn't like that, either.

Plus, I still remember how hard it was to be alone. At the beginning of this school year, I didn't have any of the friends I do now, and I'm sure kids like Josh Blues and Nadia made fun of me.

I pulled my sandwich out of my bag and snuck a look back over at Wilu.

Then I looked back at my friends and took a bite out of my sandwich. Everyone was laughing and talking about Allana and Dale being covered in slime.

A friendly voice said, "What are you guys talking about?"

I turned around and saw that it

was Mary Ann, standing with our other friend, Jenny.

She and Jenny had wanted to be part of our group costume, too, and they did not disappoint:

I was about to tell Mary Ann that we were talking about the mess Allana and Dale had made that morning, but Allana said something else.

"Hey, check out the new kid in our class," Allana said, and pointed to Wilu.

"You mean the cute new boy everyone's talking about?" Jenny asked.

That made everyone look over at Wilu again.

Except Sammy, whose cheeks turned the color of raspberries.

And except me, who didn't need to look back at him a third

time. I knew what Wilu looked like.

I didn't even have time to think about whether he might be cute or not because Mary Ann asked, "Aww, why's he sitting alone?"

Then I guess my stick-up-for-the-new-kid feelings mixed in with my being-alone-stinks feelings, because I said, "You know what, that's a good point. Let's go over there."

"But we asked him, and he didn't want to sit with us," Sammy said.

"Maybe he didn't know whether we were friendly. We can show him that we are now," I said.

"I'll go with you," Mary Ann said.

"You're just going over there because he's cute," Jenny said.

Mary Ann smiled and shook her head. But she didn't say how she felt. "Come with us," she said.

Jenny's cheeks matched Sammy's. "I'll stay here," she said.

Allana and Dale nodded.

We wanna meet
And sit with Wilu
So we can rap
About him too
It's not good to rap
About someone
If you don't know them
From a piece of bacon

My stomach gurgled. "You had to mention bacon! Can we please go over there so we can finish our lunches before my stomach explodes?"

LJ laughed. "Your stomach is always about to explode," she said. "But yeah, I'll join you guys too."

Sammy sighed sadly.

"You're just going to end up back here," Nadia said. "If he didn't want to sit with us earlier, that's not going to change two seconds later."

I ignored Nadia and packed up my lunch.

Allana, Dale, Mary Ann, LJ,

and I all headed over to Wilu's table.

"Hey, Wilu. Can we sit with you?" asked LJ.

Wilu just stared at us and didn't say a word.

"I'll take that as a yes," I said, and sat down.

The rest of the Wilu Welcoming Committee followed my lead, sitting down and unpacking their lunches.

"I'm Mary Ann. I'm in the other fifth grade class."

"Is that the honors class?" Wilu asked.

"No...," Mary Ann said. She picked at her sandwich crust. "I wouldn't be in the honors class."

"There is no honors class," Allana said.

"Not that we'd be in it, either," Dale said.

"That makes sense," Wilu said.

His words surprised me. They sounded kind of mean.

"What are you saying?" I asked. "You don't think we're smart enough to be in honors classes?"

"I don't know enough about you to say that," Wilu said. "I just thought I'd be in one. So I wondered if I was in the wrong class."

Everyone was quiet.

But LJ broke the silence with a perfect sports question.

"So, if you're really into soccer, do you like the World Cup?"

"I do," he said.

We all looked at him, waiting for him to say more. I thought for sure he'd tell us about his favorite teams, like he had in class. I mean, if he wasn't going to talk about soccer, which he'd already said he liked a lot, then what could we possibly do to get him to talk to us?

But…yeah. Wilu just sat there. Eating some kind of muffin and beef jerky, I think.

LJ wasn't going to give up.

"My brother says England is the one to beat."

Wilu nodded his head.

"But he says Croatia's going to want to come back with a fury like no other."

Wilu kept nodding his head.

Then I did something that I didn't expect again.

Usually, when I do something because I'm a little angry, I feel bad about it afterward. In the moment, I start to feel warm, even hot sometimes, and I just explode.

This time, I didn't feel hot. And I didn't feel bad about it later, either.

Maybe it's because I was just confused, so it wasn't really anger. Maybe not understanding the situation made me feel like I did the right thing.

I pulled my hood up (which was hard to do with my hat on) and said, "What is with you?"

Everyone's eyes snapped toward me. Including Wilu's.

"Robin!" Mary Ann said.

"No," I said. "He's being rude. He says how much he likes soccer, and then LJ tries to talk to him about it, and he doesn't say a word. You try to introduce yourself, and he has to make sure we know he thinks he's smarter than us. We're trying to be nice to you. I just don't understand why you won't be nice back."

A smile the size of a grain of rice slid across Wilu's face and then disappeared.

"Look, it's not that you guys

aren't friendly. You seem fine. It's just...I know how this goes." He took a bite of his muffin and then kept talking. "You guys will be nice to me while I'm here, and then I'll leave, because my mom will get sent off to Rhode Island or some other state, and then I'll never hear from you again."

Wilu looked down at his food. "It happens every time," he whispered. He looked back up at us and started to pack up his lunch without even looking at it. "So, I'm sure you're nice, but I'm a solo kid. I have to be."

Then he stood up and left the

table. Everyone watched him walk
away.

I put my hood down, and the
most surprising thing of all popped
into my head:

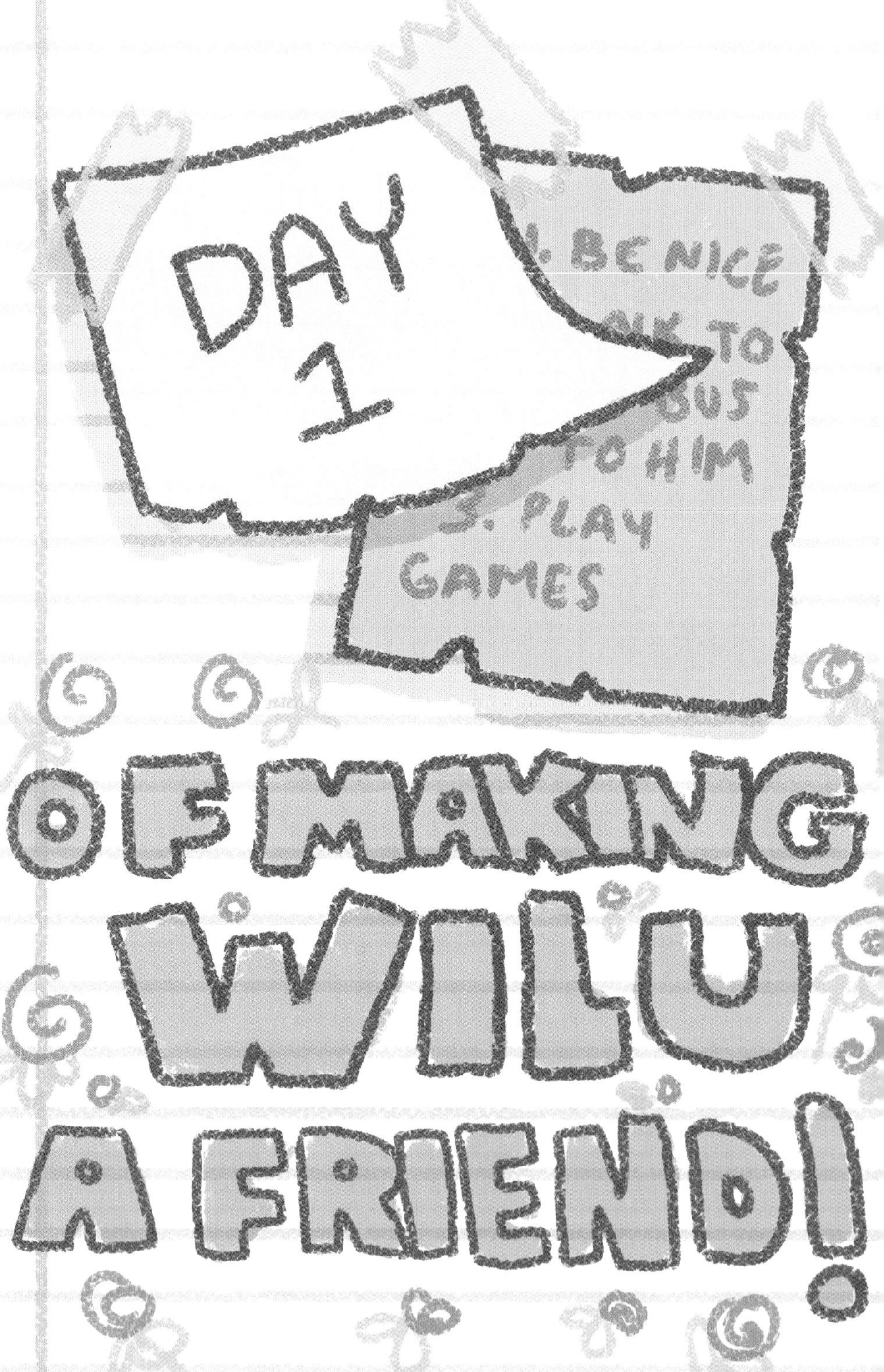
DAY 1
BE NICE
ALK TO
BUS
TO HIM
3. PLAY
GAMES
OF MAKING WILU A FRIEND!

CHAPTER 4

Before we could get outside for recess, Ms. Harrison, who's the recess aide, and Principal Roberta stopped us by the exit. Principal Roberta was dressed as a vampire, and Ms. Harrison was dressed in a big penguin suit.

"We have a little surprise for you," Principal Roberta said. "You're all going to pass through, one at a time, as we hand you these bags. And I want you all to thank Ms. Harrison because she arranged this special treat for you!"

Everyone shuffled forward, and Principal Roberta handed me a small black tote bag.

"Happy Halloween, Robin," Principal Roberta said.

"You too," I said. "Thank you for the surprise."

"I hope you like it," she said.

I stepped outside and could not believe my eyes!

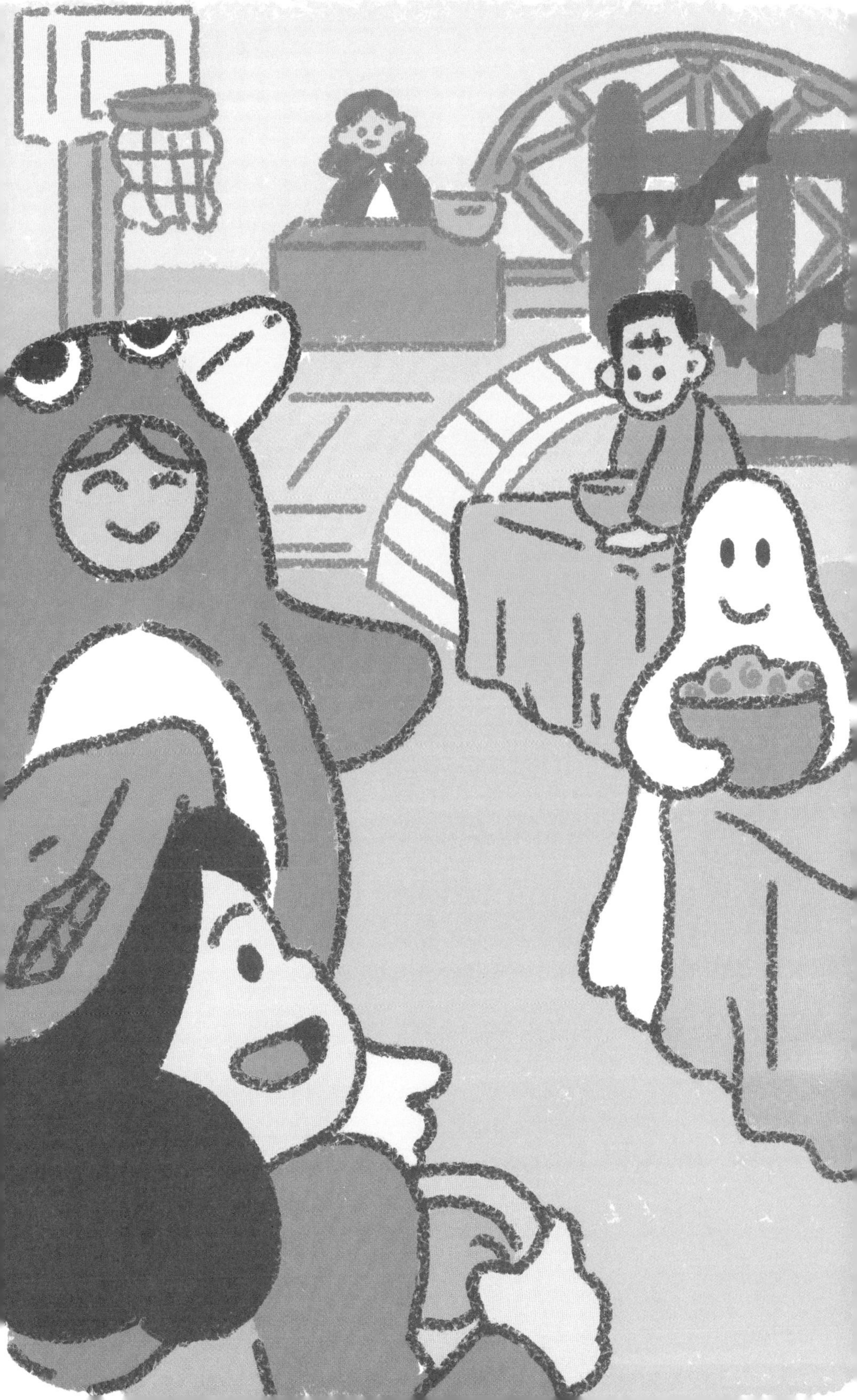

Ms. Harrison had created a recess trick-or-treat for us.

And it. Was. AWESOME!

In the middle of it all, I told LJ my plan to make friends with Wilu.

"I'm up for the challenge," she said. "He reminds me of Nadia."

I nodded. They were both tough, and Nadia had been a loner at one time, too.

We looked around so we could get started on our plan, but there were so many kids that we couldn't find Wilu anywhere.

Then, when we got back to Ms. Gaffey's room, something kind of odd happened.

We were all in the classroom talking to each other, until someone heard a knock on the door.

"Who could that be?" Dale asked as he turned around.

Sammy looked at the window in the door. "It's Ms. Gaffey."

He went to the locked door and opened it for her.

"Thank you, Sammy," she said. She went over to her desk. "Let me give you two Bonus Bucks for being so kind."

By the way, none of this was the weird part. Sammy's always super helpful with Ms. Gaffey. It's what happened next that was strange.

"Oh no, it looks like I don't have any more bucks," Ms. Gaffey said. She shuffled around the items in her desk. "That's funny—I thought I had more in here."

"Does . . . ," Sammy started to say, and then stopped. He whispered, "Does that mean I don't get any bucks?"

"I'm sorry, Sammy. Not today. But I really do appreciate you opening the door for me."

I felt sorry for Sammy, but I figured Ms. Gaffey would get more bucks tomorrow, and I focused back on the really exciting stuff.

Like Halloween afternoon . . .

We killed it at the costume contest.

Ms. Decker, the librarian, read us a not-too-scary ghost story.

And we watched a scary-but-not-too-scary movie.

But at the end of the day, I didn't forget my new mission. I walked over to Wilu while he was waiting in line for the bus, and I tapped him on the shoulder.

"Hey," I said. "I hope you had a nice first day of school."

He shrugged, and I turned to walk away, but then I heard him say, "Thanks."

I smiled and headed to my line.

Then another really, *really* odd thing happened to me that made me rethink the whole Ms. Gaffey thing.

Nadia ran over to me and yelled, "What are you doing?!?!"

"I was just—"

"You can't talk to Wilu anymore!"

I looked at her like she was trying to hand me a piece of pizza.

Have I made it clear how much I don't like pizza? No? Yuck!

Anyway, with my face all scrunched up, I asked, "Why not?"

"Isn't it obvious?" she said. "Wilu stole the Bonus Bucks from Ms. Gaffey!"

DAY 2

ADDING ANOTHER OUTLAW?

RESULTS UNCLEAR

CHAPTER 5

TUESDAY, NOVEMBER 1

The whole bus ride home yesterday, all I could think about was what Nadia had said to me.

"You don't think it's weird that the first day Ms. Gaffey can't find her Bonus Bucks is the same day Wilu starts school?" Nadia had asked.

I had shrugged my shoulders and run to catch my bus.

Sure, my gut had felt weird when I first saw Wilu, and I couldn't figure him out. But after he told us that kids always just drop him as a friend the second his parents have to move to a new town for work, I felt kind of bad for him.

Nadia hadn't wanted to give Wilu a chance, so she hadn't been at his lunch table when he said that. She didn't know any of that stuff, but I did, and I wasn't going to start thinking he was stealing bucks based on Nadia's opinion.

So on the bus ride to school today, I decided to totally ignore what Nadia had said.

Yeah, she'd turned over a new leaf and seemed to be much nicer, but this was just another example of the two of us butting heads.

Plus, my weird feelings aren't always something I can trust. And when Wilu explained that he didn't think it was worth making friends, all the stuff I'd thought was odd about him at first actually made sense.

For me, that's when I decided

I wanted to prove him wrong. Kids in other schools may have given up on being friends with him when he moved away, but I don't think that was fair to Wilu. Everyone deserves friends.

And I definitely wasn't going to start accusing him of stealing the bucks.

When I walked into Ms. Gaffey's classroom, Nadia locked eyes with me right away. Even though she was just looking at me, it felt like she was doing this:

But I broke the stare and deliberately walked past Wilu's desk before I went to mine.

"Hey, Wilu. What's up?" I asked as I passed him.

He nodded his head once at me, and I headed to my desk.

When I got there, LJ and Allana were whispering to each other across their desks. They broke apart and waved me in.

"Did Nadia tell you her theory about Wilu and the Bonus Bucks?" Allana asked me.

"Yeah," I said. "But I don't buy it."

"Me neither," LJ said. "Doesn't seem likely."

"It's what Dale and I are rapping about today," Allana said.

"About Wilu?" I asked.

She shook her head. "Just the bucks."

Then she turned her head to Dale and he nodded his head.

But before they could even start, the mystery around the missing Bonus Bucks got even more mysterious.

Ms. Gaffey opened her desk and said, "Well that's odd."

"What's wrong, Ms. Gaffey?" Josh asked.

Ms. Gaffey held her hand up like this:

"I picked up more Bonus Bucks from Principal Roberta this morning, but I'm missing at least thirty Bonus Bucks from my pile. I guess I'll have to be a little more stringent with my disbursement today. Ah! Let's define those words I just used..."

My jaw dropped. I don't know why, but I looked over at Nadia.

Nadia tipped her head toward Wilu
and shook her head back and forth.

But she might as well have been
doing this:

Just then, there was a knock at the door. Ms. Gaffey waved her hand and Principal Roberta entered.

Everyone sat up extra straight, like they were pretending their spines were all made from ears of corn. Everybody knew they were supposed to be on good behavior for Ms. Gaffey, but you had to be extra good around Principal Roberta. Plus, she didn't stop by our classroom too often. If she did, it was usually because somebody was in trouble.

Nobody looked Principal Roberta in the eye because they

were all afraid *they* were the person in trouble.

"Hello, everyone," Principal Roberta said.

The whole class answered in the same voice, facing the board. "Hello, Principal Roberta."

"How's everything going today, Ms. Gaffey?" Principal Roberta asked.

"Well, I seem to have misplaced some of my bucks, but otherwise it's going well."

But Principal Roberta didn't seem worried. She just said, "Everyone behaving themselves despite that?"

Ms. Gaffey smiled a quick smile and said, "So far."

"All right then," Principal Roberta said. "Carry on, class." Then she left the room.

If Principal Roberta didn't seem worried that Ms. Gaffey's Bonus Bucks were gone, then I wasn't going to worry, either. After all, if our school principal didn't think it was a big deal, why should any of us?

Besides, LJ and I had a bigger mission with Wilu. We were going to make him our bestie.

Or, you know, just get him to laugh and talk to us. That'd be fine too.

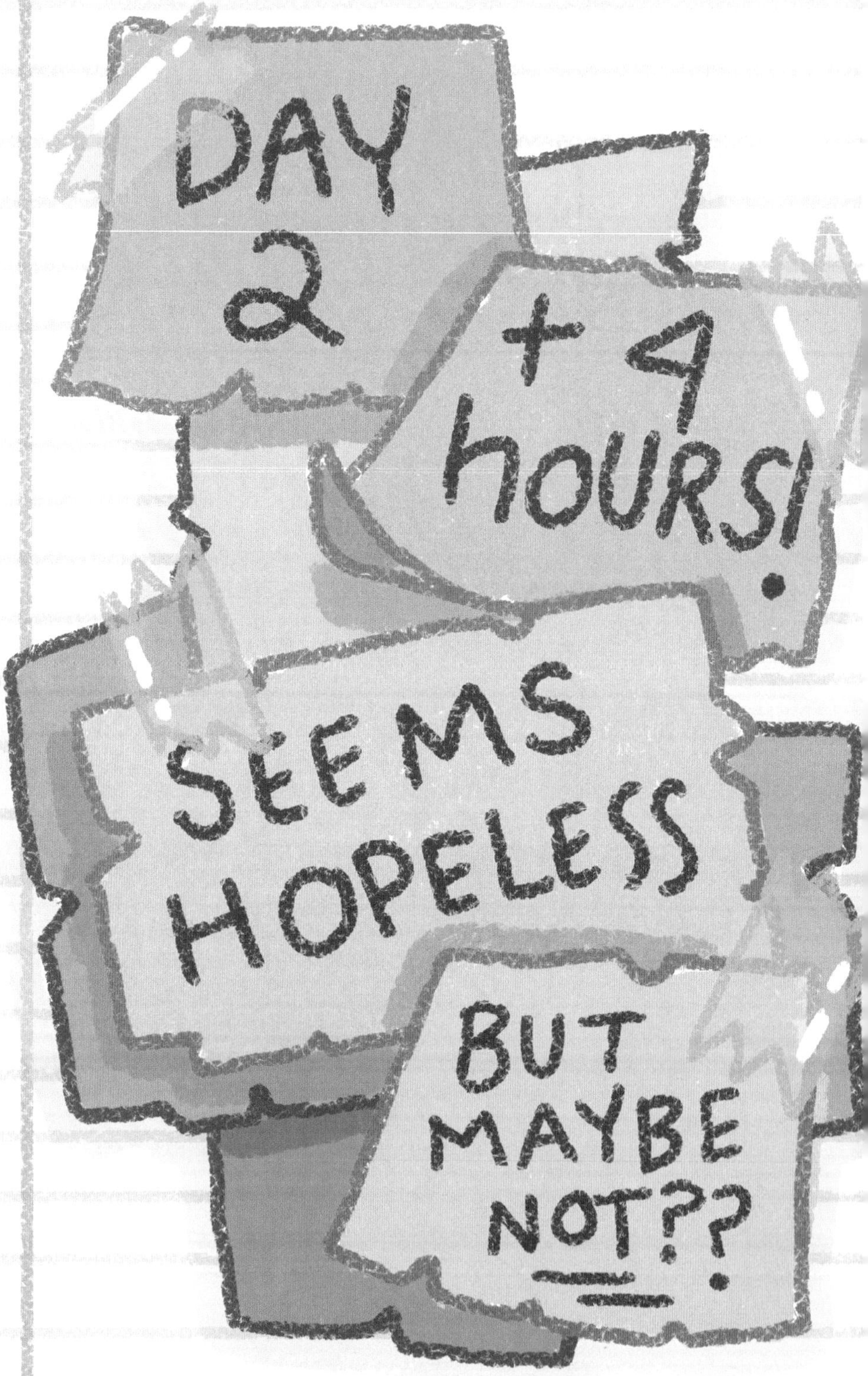
DAY 2
+ 4 HOURS!
SEEMS HOPELESS
BUT MAYBE NOT??

CHAPTER 6

So far, LJ's and my plan to get Wilu to talk to us was getting more and more difficult by the hour.

Yeah, he'd said he didn't want any friends, but we were pretty sure that if we kept at it, we'd break down that wall.

We asked him to join our science group, but he said he wanted to work solo.

We thought he'd like gym class, but that was a dud.

17! William Shakespeare! Quatrains! MLK Jr.! 3,789! Sonnets! I Have a Dream!

The only time he seemed happy was when he was answering Ms. Gaffey's questions.

While I was hoping that Wilu's wall was made of something kind of sturdy, but also kind of easy to break, like a graham cracker, it turned out it was more like my mom's mac and cheese. (Don't go near it unless you want to chip a tooth!)

I could tell LJ was starting to give up hope, but I tried to keep her spirits up.

"So maybe he's just a harder nut to crack," I said as we walked to lunch. "Like a walnut instead of a peanut. Doesn't mean we can't crack it. It just means it'll take longer than we thought."

LJ nodded her head, but she didn't look at me.

"I'm going to sit with my cousin today," Nadia said. She waved bye and walked toward the other side of the cafeteria.

Mary Ann and Jenny were already at the lunch table. I watched as Wilu walked to an empty table and sat alone again.

Then Mary Ann turned and said, "Something weird happened in our class today."

"Super extra weird," Jenny said.

"What happened?" Sammy asked.

"Our teacher, Ms. Hammond,

was going to give Freddy Smyth some Bonus Bucks for offering to clean up the art table," Mary Ann said. "Which is a little weird because Freddy usually makes messes, not cleans them up."

"Tell them what we were talking about!" Jenny said. Then she looked around and whispered, "About Nadia!"

"In a minute," Mary Ann said. "Ms. Hammond went to give Freddy some bucks, but they were gone."

Allana, Dale, Sammy, LJ, and I all looked at each other.

"That happened in our class too," LJ said.

Mary Ann and Jenny looked at each other.

I guess if I thought about it, Ms. Gaffey losing things wasn't too odd, but the fact that it was Bonus Bucks was a little strange. And knowing she wasn't the only teacher losing bucks definitely made it a lot stranger.

But then I realized just what Mary Ann had said.

"Wait, didn't you say something about Nadia?" I asked.

Mary Ann's cheeks turned the color of beets.

"Well...Jenny and I were talking...and I hate to say it...but what if Nadia is stealing the bucks?"

LJ shook her head. "Come on," she said. "That's not fair."

"Nadia thinks Wilu is taking them," Sammy said.

Mary Ann and Jenny looked at each other.

"What?" I asked.

"Well . . . that was our other theory," Jenny said.

I shook my head like I'd shake a tree branch to get an apple down.

"Don't blame him," I said.

"So you think it's Nadia, then," Mary Ann said.

"She didn't say that," LJ said.

"But it makes sense," Mary Ann said. "Nadia would totally blame Wilu if it was really her taking them."

"LJ," Sammy said, and turned around to face Wilu's table. "If it's not Nadia…do you think it could be Wilu?"

"I…," she started, and looked at me. I shook my head again. If there was any part of LJ that wasn't sure about Wilu, I didn't want it to convince her that he was guilty without any proof.

It must have worked, because she said, "I don't know what's happening, but I don't think we

82

should go pointing fingers."

Jenny turned to me and said, "But Robin, you must see that it could be Nadia, right?"

That wasn't an easy question for me to answer.

The last time I'd thought Nadia was up to no good, all she'd really wanted was a friend. My gut instinct had been completely wrong.

But I still didn't think Nadia was some totally good kid.

I also didn't think anyone should blame Wilu. I was pretty sure that my gut had been wrong about him too.

"I don't think it was Nadia," I said. "But I don't think it's Wilu, either. And I'm really not comfortable with everyone blaming people. We don't know enough about the situation to say who's stealing the bucks."

I stood up and pointed to Wilu's table. "Anyway, I'm going to tell Wilu he should join us at recess."

Allana and Dale looked at each other and nodded their heads.

You should probably
Just leave him alone
If you ask him to play
He'll probably just groan

84

He's a "solo kid"
   That means just one
If you get too close
   He might just run!

LJ and Jenny giggled. LJ saw my face and stopped right away.

I put my hood up.

"That's not very nice," I said. "I thought you used your raps to be funny in a kind way."

The twins looked at each other and then down at the table. "Sorry, Robin," Allana said. "We were trying to bc funny, not mean."

"Yeah, but you two heard him," I continued. "He stays by himself because he keeps losing friends every time his family moves. LJ and I were trying to show him that things can be different here."

I looked over at Wilu. "And *I'm* still going to try."

I walked to Wilu's table.

My friends were all confusing me. Why did Allana and Dale tease Wilu with that rap? Was it because they didn't understand him? Did they think he was the person stealing bucks?

And why had LJ giggled? Didn't she say she wanted to help me try and make friends with him?

And why would Mary Ann and

Jenny think he was the one stealing bucks? Just yesterday, Jenny thought he was the cute new boy, and now she thought he might be stealing from teachers.

And they also thought it could be Nadia. And this was just after last week, when they all thought I was taking it too far by accusing Nadia of being mean.

Everything about my friends felt like it was changing every day, and I didn't quite know how to keep up.

But there was one thing I did know how to do.

And that was to be myself.

"Hey, Wilu," I said as I put my hands on either side of his lunch table. "We're playing kickball at recess, if you want to join us."

He looked at me sideways.

"Why are you trying so hard to be my friend?"

"I'm just letting you know we're playing kickball. No one said anything about making you be my friend." Then I walked back to my lunch table.

Okay, yes, I was trying to get him to be my friend. But I have a pretty good feeling that if I just tell Wilu over and over again that he should be my friend, that's not going to change his mind.

After all, I've learned that friends are earned. And I want to earn his friendship. I just have to prove to him that I am worth being friends with.

Hopefully, I will be better at that than my mom is at making mac and cheese. (Okay, Mom, I know you read this, so I'm sorry. But maybe let Dad try his hand at it?)

I was hoping, since nobody brought up the stolen bucks for the rest of lunch, that we could all forget about them for a little while and just have a fun recess.

I thought that we could just play kickball, and maybe Wilu would join us and everything would start to come together.

But...yeah. My hopes should have been a lot lower.

Wilu did join us, but that's not how recess started. It started with us getting a kickball and heading to the field, but the whole time, Nadia talked about Ms. Hammond's stolen bucks.

"So, I told Aaron, 'You know we have a new kid in class, and I bet it's him.'"

"Let's pick teams," I said, ignoring Nadia. "LJ, you want to be the other captain?"

LJ nodded and stood next to me.

But Nadia wasn't quitting. "Robin!" she yelled. "You need to hear this whole thing."

"Why?" I said. "Why do I need to hear anything about the stolen bucks?"

"Because," Nadia said, "you're

The Outlaw, aren't you? You're the one trying to get kids their bucks back. That's why you stole them from me, isn't it?"

I'd had the kickball in my hand, but I dropped it when she said that.

I knew Nadia was trying not to be the same person, but when she was being all bossy in this moment, and bringing up that LJ and I stole bucks from her because she was being so mean on the playground . . . well, those things made it hard to forget that she could be such a bully.

"I thought that since bucks are missing from teachers' desks, you'd want to do something about it," Nadia continued. "But maybe you only stole the bucks from me because you wanted it to look like you were doing the right thing, when really it was just that you didn't like me."

Then Nadia stormed off.

I didn't know what to say. I tried yelling, "Nadia, wait!" But Nadia didn't stop. She stomped her feet into the ground and kept going.

I knew Nadia wasn't totally right. We didn't even know if the bucks were being stolen.

Principal Roberta had been in our classroom and had heard

that Ms. Gaffey was missing bucks, and she didn't seem worried about it. She had probably seen Ms. Hammond too.

And Mary Ann and Jenny hadn't said anything about Principal Roberta thinking it was odd.

In fact, they hadn't mentioned her stopping by at all, which meant it was probably no big deal in their classroom, either.

To me, that meant it wasn't something I had to worry about.

So why did Nadia think it was? Why was she making such a big stink about it?

I shook my head and turned away from her. She was wrong. She just couldn't see it.

And I knew all too well what that was like.

She was going to have to figure out how wrong she was on her own. That's what happened to me.

Then Wilu came over and said, "Did you already pick teams?"

I looked at Wilu and smiled. He actually came over! Maybe he was willing to see that things could be different for him at Nottingham Elementary. It also felt pretty good to know that putting extra effort into being nice to someone might actually make them feel welcome, after all.

I patted him on the back. "We only just started. Want to be on my team?"

Wilu nodded and stood next to Sammy.

While LJ picked Dale, I heard Wilu ask Sammy, "Why did Nadia leave?"

"Oh, it doesn't matter," Sammy said.

I smiled to myself. At least Sammy wasn't jumping on the "blame Wilu" train that everyone else was.

And for the rest of recess,

nobody talked about missing bucks. Nobody accused anybody of anything. And Wilu played kickball with us the whole time.

I think that's the moment his shell cracked just a tiny bit.

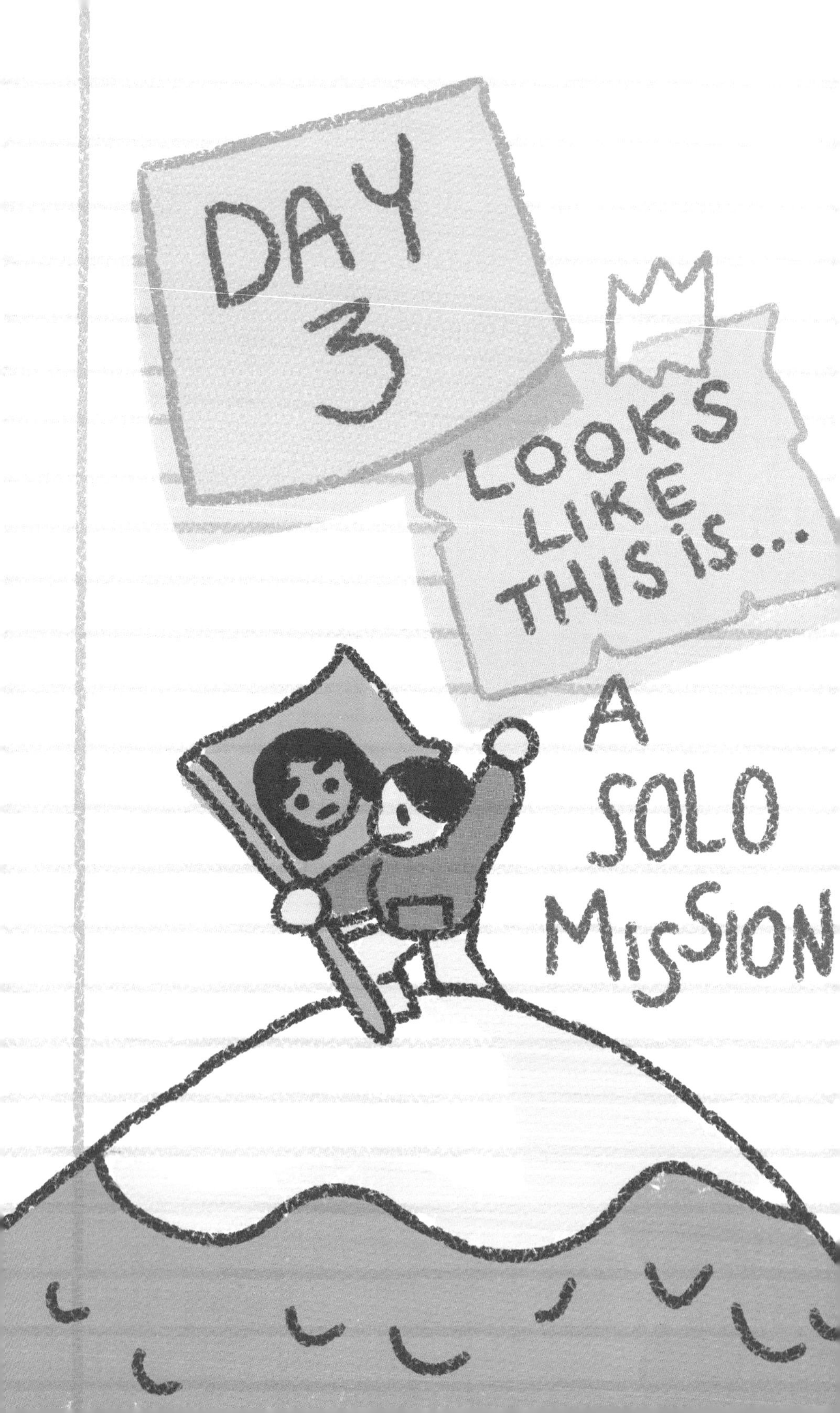
DAY 3
LOOKS LIKE THIS IS...
A SOLO MISSION

CHAPTER 7

WEDNESDAY, NOVEMBER 2

Even though we had a pretty perfect recess yesterday, the rest of the day ended with a lot of kids in our class frustrated about Ms. Gaffey not having enough bucks to give out.

On the way to school today, I was thinking about how those kids were reacting.

My classmates didn't seem to mind not getting bucks for doing good things around the classroom, but not getting bucks for good grades really bugged some kids.

YOU'RE SAYING I DON'T GET <u>ANY</u> BUCKS FOR THESE?

Still, without Nadia's unfair playground tax, kids shouldn't really be worried about whether they have enough bucks or not.

Yeah, Principal Roberta has cool prizes, and they'll be harder to get if bucks aren't being given out so freely. I could see why kids were bummed that they couldn't win them as fast as they could before.

But it's not like they can't still get them. It had turned into more of a raffle system. Sometimes you got them, sometimes you didn't.

I didn't think it was a big deal to not get as many.

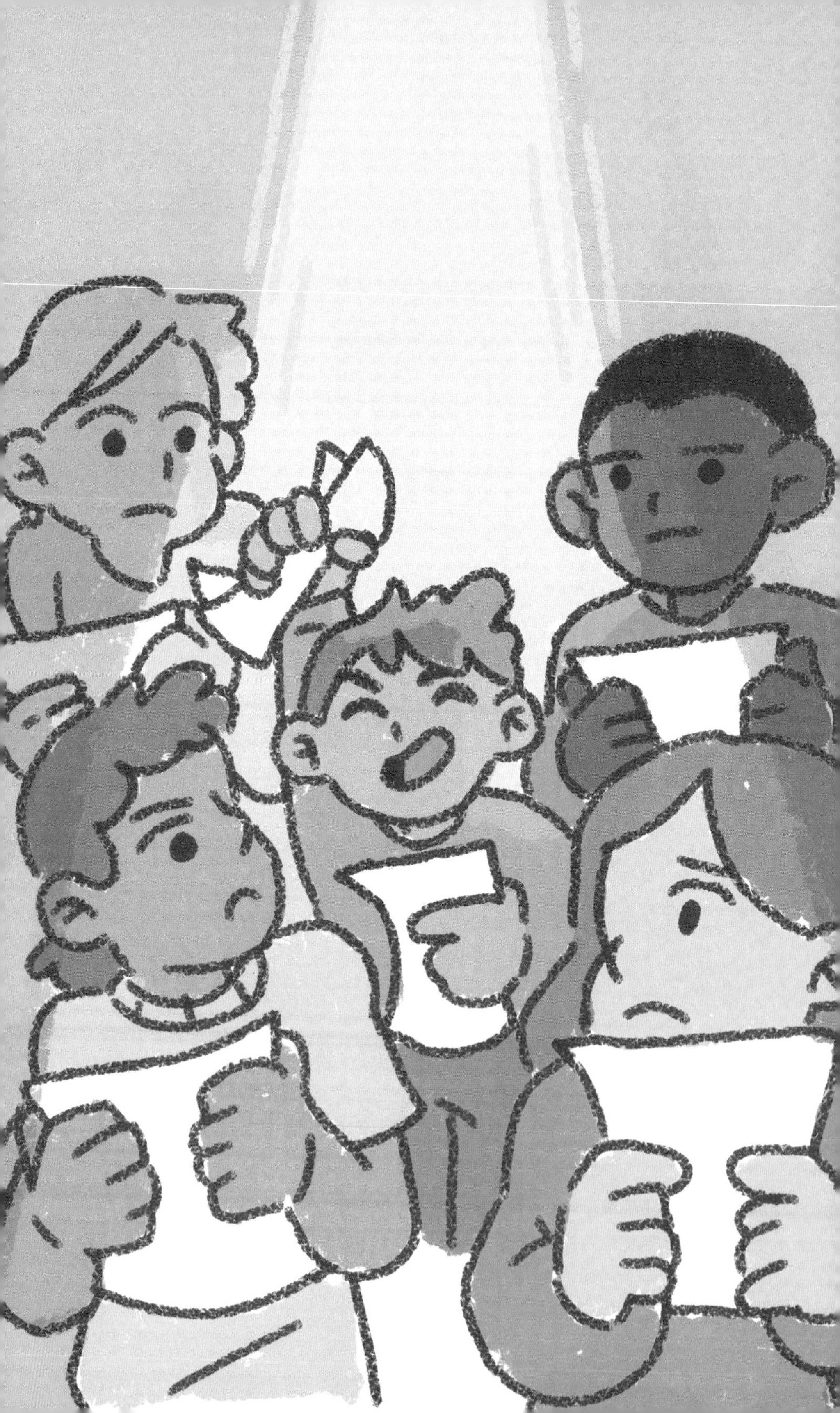

Maybe I didn't mind because
I didn't usually get bucks for my
grades, because mine are only okay.

And even though I did usually
get bucks for doing nice things, I
did those things because they were
the right thing to do, not because it
meant that I would get bucks.

Plus, if the teachers and
Principal Roberta weren't worried
about the missing bucks, why
should we be worried? My gut told
me something was up, but I knew
I had to ignore that feeling. All
of my other thoughts made more
sense.

But...yeah. It turned out

that other people were way more bothered by all this bucks craziness than I was. When I walked into class today, everyone was whispering like wild.

I said hi to Wilu, and he waved back.

The second I got to my seat, LJ leaned over her desk and tapped me on the shoulder. "So, you want to hear something crazy?"

"Shoot," I said.

Allana and Dale nodded to each other, but I held up my hand before they could begin.

"If this is another mean rap about Wilu, I don't want to hear it."

The twins blushed at the same time. "No," Allana said. "It was about something we heard."

I had a feeling it wasn't going to be good news and it would have to do with Wilu anyway, so I said, "How about you just tell me?"

"Okay," Dale said. "Apparently, it's not just fifth grade teachers who are missing bucks."

Allana nodded. "Mr. Dunken, the fourth grade teacher, didn't have all his bucks yesterday."

"And Ms. Bough—she teaches third grade—told her class she couldn't find a bunch of her bucks," she said.

Allana and Dale looked at each other.

"Can we at least do the end of the rap?" Dale asked.

I sighed. "Sure."

With all of these
Missing bucks
We bet someone
Is loading up their truck
So they can count
All their dough
And then use the truck
To make tacos!

I smiled and sat down in my seat. It was a good rap, but I really didn't want to talk about the bucks anymore.

And the twins mentioning tacos just made me want to eat like fifteen tacos as soon as possible.

With extra salsa.

And extra queso fresco.

To be honest, I was really sick of talking about bucks altogether. But I seemed to be the only one.

LJ leaned back in her seat. "It's a little suspicious, isn't it?"

"I guess," I said and turned to face LJ. "But I don't think it means anything."

LJ looked at Wilu and then back at me, raising her eyebrow.

My mouth actually dropped open. I couldn't believe what she was suggesting.

"You don't think Wilu is the problem, do you?" I asked.

LJ shrugged. "I'm not convinced...but it makes some sense."

I shook my head. "Not you, too!"

"Hear me out," she said. "Who's better to sneak into classrooms and steal bucks than the kid who wants to be totally left alone?"

I blocked her thoughts from coming into my head like I blocked my vegetables from touching my noodles.

"No way," I said. "He hasn't even been alone that much. We've been getting him to hang out with us."

"Robin, put your Outlaw cap back on. Nadia was right yesterday. Something like this would normally bother you. Why isn't it bothering you now?"

I turned back around and stared at the board.

How could I explain all of my reasons to LJ?

I'd thought we were being outlaws by getting Wilu to join our Merry Misfit gang. He'd made it pretty clear why he keeps to himself. Had everyone forgotten what he'd said?

Was I just all mixed up again?

I didn't know what to think anymore, except this: Fifth grade is the most confusing year yet.

By lunch, the rumors were flying around the cafeteria. There were the whispers about how the first and second grade classrooms were missing bucks now, too. And there were lots of stories that it was all Wilu's fault.

When I sat down at the lunch table, I was hoping that everyone would start talking about

Thanksgiving already. I was going to say, "Hey, who else's mouth waters when they think about potato stuffing?"

But...after this moment, I decided to stop thinking anything about anything and just let my brain go blank.

Because nobody had any interest in turkey or cranberries or even potato stuffing.

That's right—EVEN POTATO STUFFING!

Nadia was in the middle of a speech on why Wilu was clearly the person stealing all of the bucks.

"...LJ made a very good point. Sure, he played kickball with you guys yesterday. But where was he between lunch and when he came over to us? Nobody knows. Nobody saw him."

"That's because he keeps to himself," I said.

Nadia shook her head. "Nope. It's because he was off in the classrooms, stealing bucks from teachers."

"Don't the teachers lock the doors during lunch?" I asked.

"Remember, Ms. Gaffey needed Sammy to open it the other day because she kept it locked longer than usual."

"Maybe he knows how to pick locks," Jenny said.

Everyone nodded their head. Even Sammy and Mary Ann.

"What?" I said. "You all believe that?" I turned to Mary Ann. "I thought you felt bad because he was all by himself?"

"I did at first," she said. "But it all adds up, Robin." Mary Ann leaned closer to me. "I should have gotten six Bonus Bucks today. And I didn't get any. That's not fair."

"Just because it's not fair doesn't mean it's Wilu's fault," I said. "And you know, yesterday you thought it might be Nadia."

I turned to Nadia, thinking she'd be all red-faced and nervous, but she was as cool as an ice cube.

"I know kids thought it was me," she said. "But that's why I'm helping them see that it's Wilu. Because I'm not like that anymore. But we don't know what this Wilu kid is like."

"No, YOU don't know what he's like," I said. "I'm starting to get to know him, and he's nice."

"Is he, though?" LJ asked. "He's

saying he doesn't have any friends because they don't keep in touch with him. But what if they don't keep in touch with him because he's not very nice?"

That was the last comment I could sit there and hear.

Especially when it came from LJ.

I shot out of my seat. I felt all the heat in my body rise up like this:

I had been nice and had tried to talk to them calmly about this, but nobody was listening. So I was done.

I took in a deep breath, put my hood up, and spit out all of what I said next as one big sentence.

"You know, just last week I tried to convince all of you that Nadia was being mean, and I was totally wrong, and you all helped me see how wrong I was, and now, nobody really knows Wilu, and it's not fair to just blame something weird on him and make up stuff like we think that he's not very nice, and if you all think it's him who stole the bucks, I think you're all pretty mean, and I'm going to go sit with him until you all realize how wrong you are."

I grabbed my lunch and turned around. But then I turned back to say one more thing.

"And LJ, I'm really the most sad about you. We were going to work together to be his friend. That was supposed to be the Outlaw thing to do. And you're doing the exact opposite now!"

I walked off before she could respond. If she had something to say to me, she could follow me over to Wilu's table.

When I sat down and unpacked my lunch for the second time today, Wilu gave me a strange look.

"Why are you sitting here?"

"My friends aren't being too friendly today," I said as I took a bite of my sandwich.

"You sure that makes you want to sit with The Bucks Bandit?"

I looked up from my sandwich. "Seriously?" I asked.

"Oh yeah," he said. "The whispers in this cafeteria could wake the dead. And when no one is talking to you, it's pretty easy to hear what everyone is saying about you."

"Well," I said. "I *know* it's not you."

Wilu raised his head. "How do you know?"

"I just do."

Okay, I honestly had no idea if Wilu took the bucks.

But I also had no idea if he hadn't. And to me, that was reason enough to sit with him and eat my sandwich in peace.

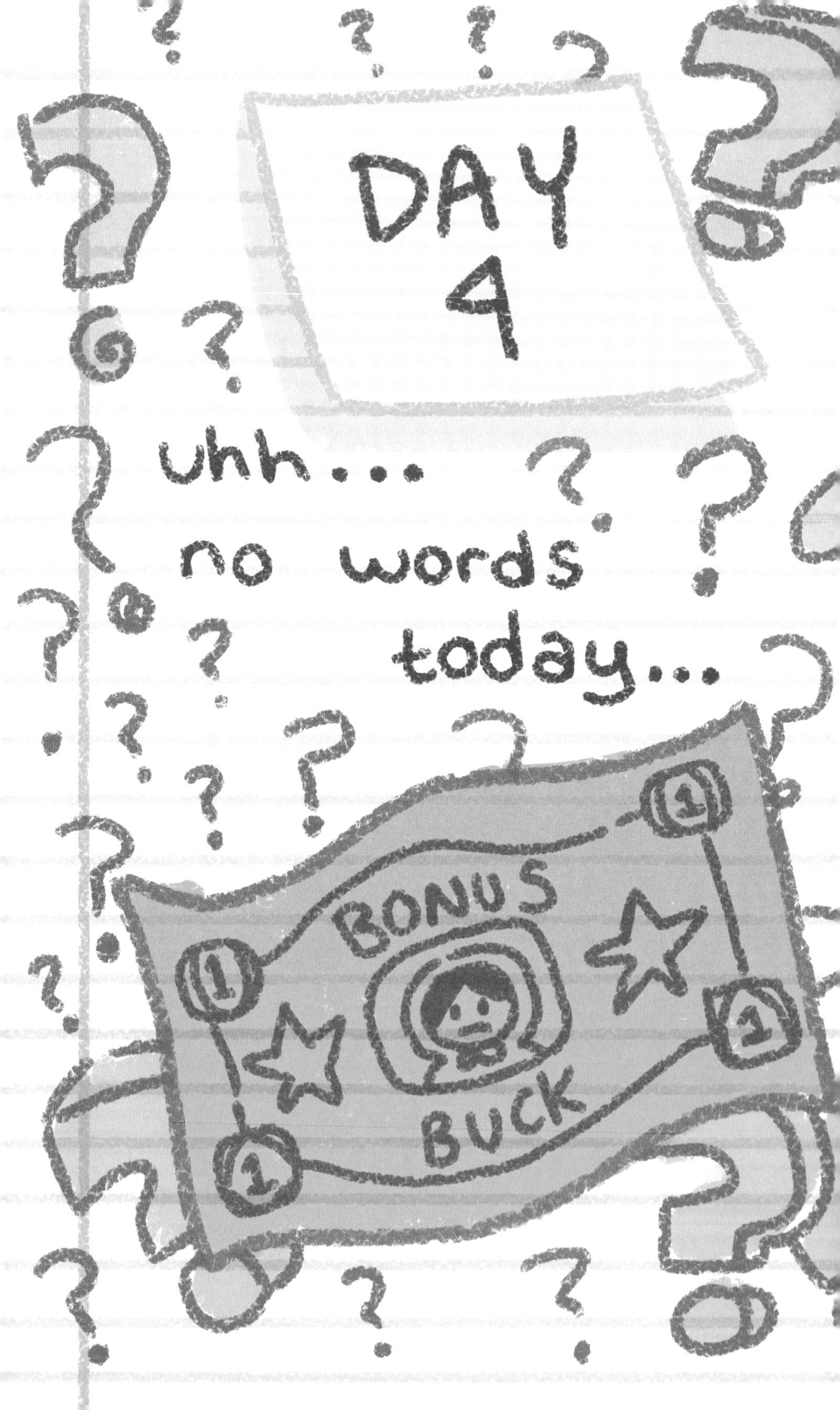

DAY 4
uhh... no words today...
BONUS BUCK
1
1
1
1

CHAPTER 8

Yesterday at recess, I finally got what I was hoping for: no Bonus Bucks talk whatsoever.

I didn't get to hang out with any of my friends because I guess

121

they were all still convinced that Wilu was the Bucks Ban—eek. I shouldn't even write that down. After calling Nadia a bully so much lately, and everyone calling Wilu that made-up name, I realize that all mean nicknames are a bad call.

Well, anyway, it was just Wilu and me at recess.

It wasn't totally easy to hang out with Wilu. He had a real stony look on his face, like I was a strawberry and he was allergic to strawberries and didn't want to get too close because things could go south for him real quick if he did.

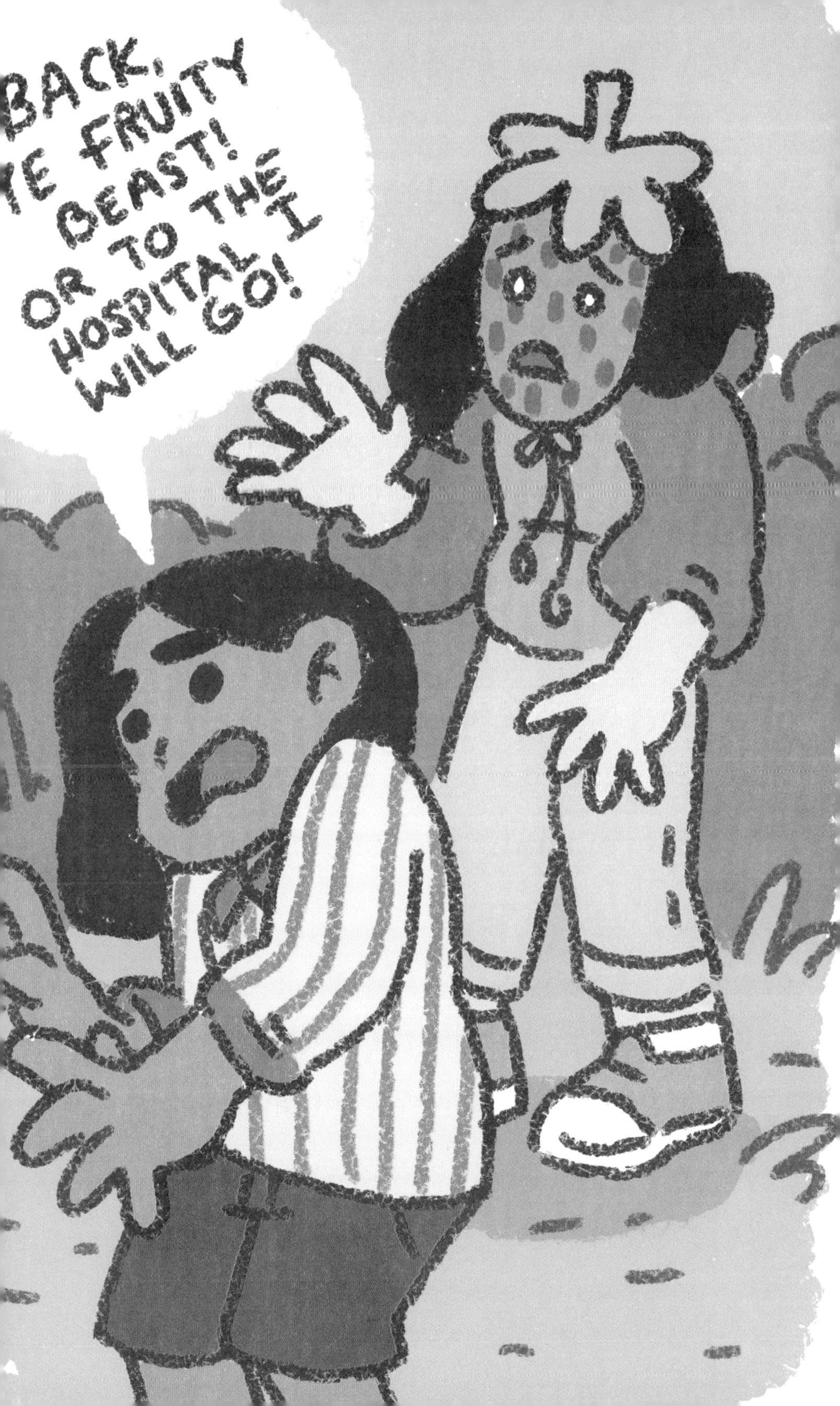
BACK, YE FRUITY BEAST! OR TO THE HOSPITAL I WILL GO!

But we walked around the blacktop together, and he told me about his little brother and how he had some cousins in different parts of the country. I told him about how I liked to fish with my dad, and it turned out that he fished sometimes too.

None of it was super deep stuff, but we were getting somewhere. I was getting to know Wilu more than the other kids had, that's for sure.

I wondered if this was what it was like when LJ became friends with Nadia. She'd had such a tough shell, so maybe she was a little cold to LJ at first, but then they started to have fun together.

Either way, I was pretty sure that by talking to him, I could make Wilu see that I was different from other kids. Maybe he'd figure out that he could let his guard down here, eventually.

And look, I also kind of hoped that if I hung out with Wilu long enough and got to know him, maybe everyone would stop giving him such a hard time.

Or maybe I'd learn that he *was* stealing the bucks, and then we'd really know, once and for all.

But either way, I knew nothing

would change without really getting to know him.

Well, until something happened today that I could never have seen coming.

Like, okay, the last few days I've been feeling all out of sorts and like I couldn't trust my gut or my friends. It made me feel like I didn't know who I was or who anyone else was anymore.

It really made me feel lonely.

I wondered if that was how Wilu felt every time he had to move. He'd wait for a call to come from an old friend, or to get an email, or to hear back from a text he sent, and then nothing ever came.

Sure, I've felt lonely before. Last week, when all my friends took Nadia's side during the big fight we were all in, and I was being a jerk, I'd felt the lowest I ever had.

But this time, with all my friends disagreeing with me, I didn't feel that low. This time, I wasn't completely alone.

This time, I had Wilu.

Well... or so I thought.

I walked down the hallway and I saw Wilu by his locker. We both put our lunches away and walked to class together. Neither of us said anything, but that didn't really throw me off.

When we walked toward Ms. Gaffey's room, I could hear everyone talking, but the second our feet landed in the classroom, the whole room went quiet.

I said, "Oooookaaaaay," and headed to my seat.

Not one second later, Ms. Gaffey came into the classroom, and Nadia jumped to her feet.

"Ms. Gaffey, the class has something to tell you!"

I didn't like the way she said that, so I jumped in. "Not the whole class," I said.

Nadia stuck out her tongue at me.

"Nadia, reel that tongue back in or I will not listen to what you have to tell me," Ms. Gaffey said.

Nadia closed her mouth and apologized while Ms. Gaffey walked to the front of the room.

"There we are," Ms. Gaffey said. "Now, what is it that the class wants to share?"

"We all know why you're missing Bonus Bucks every morning," Nadia said.

"Do you, now?" Ms. Gaffey said. She crossed her arms. "Well, I'd like to hear it."

The second Ms. Gaffey said that, the room turned into a big courtroom.

I've never been in a courtroom before, but I've seen plenty on TV.

Nadia went up to the front of the room and said, "The class believes—"

I cut her off with, "Not the whole class!"

Nadia huffed. "Everyone except Robin and Wilu believe that the reason the Bonus Bucks are gone is because Wilu stole them. We believe without shadows or doubt that it was totally him, and we have put together a case as to why we know that."

Ms. Gaffey's eyes widened.

Allana and Dale came up next, as Nadia sat back down. They looked at each other and nodded.

We believe
  Wilu stole the bucks
In every classroom
  And it totally sucks

Ms. Gaffey put her hand up to stop them. "Rhyme or not, no foul language in my classroom, you two!"

"Sorry, Ms. Gaffey," the twins said at the same time. Then they started their rap again.

Every day at recess
  We're on the playground
But where's Wilu?
  He's nowhere to be found

Sure yesterday
    He was with Robin
But other days
    You can't find him
That's when he
    Is being stealth
And stealing all
    Our hard-earned wealth
We should be
    Earning bucks
And since we're not
    It totally...

Dale paused. "Uhh...isn't cool," he said.

Ms. Gaffey looked directly at me and Wilu.

"Does anybody object to this argument?"

I stood up and walked to the front of the classroom.

By the way, none of this was the stuff that threw me for one big fruit loop!

Once I was up there, I had to think on my feet. I thought about what the twins had said and when we'd actually heard that the bucks were missing.

"To go against exactly what they said, I don't believe it's Wilu because they say he took them at recess. But lately, teachers are missing them first thing in the morning. So that doesn't really add up because I don't think he's the first kid in here in the morning."

Ms. Gaffey nodded her head.

Then, as I walked back to my desk, I saw LJ stand up and head to the front of the classroom. She didn't look me in the eye. I shook my head as she passed and sat down so hard that if my chair were a cake, I would have smashed it flat and sent it flying in twenty different directions.

I think this was the first time EVER that I wasn't hungry after thinking of cake.

LJ cleared her throat. Then she

spread her arms wide and spoke to the class. "Even when other new kids came to the school, were there issues with low amounts of bucks? And after years of earning bucks, have you ever been more disappointed than when you did a great job on a test or did something nice in class, and none of those good deeds were rewarded with bucks?"

She paused, and everyone except me and Wilu said, "NO!"

"That's right," she said. "Robin may have found a problem with our argument, but that doesn't mean that other things haven't lined up to explain why it must be Wilu."

I felt myself getting really warm again. I was so disappointed in my friends.

When they'd come to me and told me I was completely wrong about Nadia being mean, I'd listened to what they said. Yes, I'd stormed away at first, but then I'd thought about what they'd told me, and I'd realized I'd been wrong.

And then I'd gone to them and apologized for being nasty.

Apparently, none of them were going to do that.

Apparently, they'd all heard me say that I thought they should stop accusing Wilu, and they'd just ignored me. That hurt.

But, if you can believe it, none of this was the part I didn't see coming.

Everyone had made it pretty clear that they thought it was Wilu stealing bucks, so when they weren't telling me they were sorry for thinking the wrong things about Wilu, it didn't surprise me to see them tell Ms. Gaffey.

It was what happened next that really got me.

Wilu finally spoke. He said, "I have a conclusion for you!"

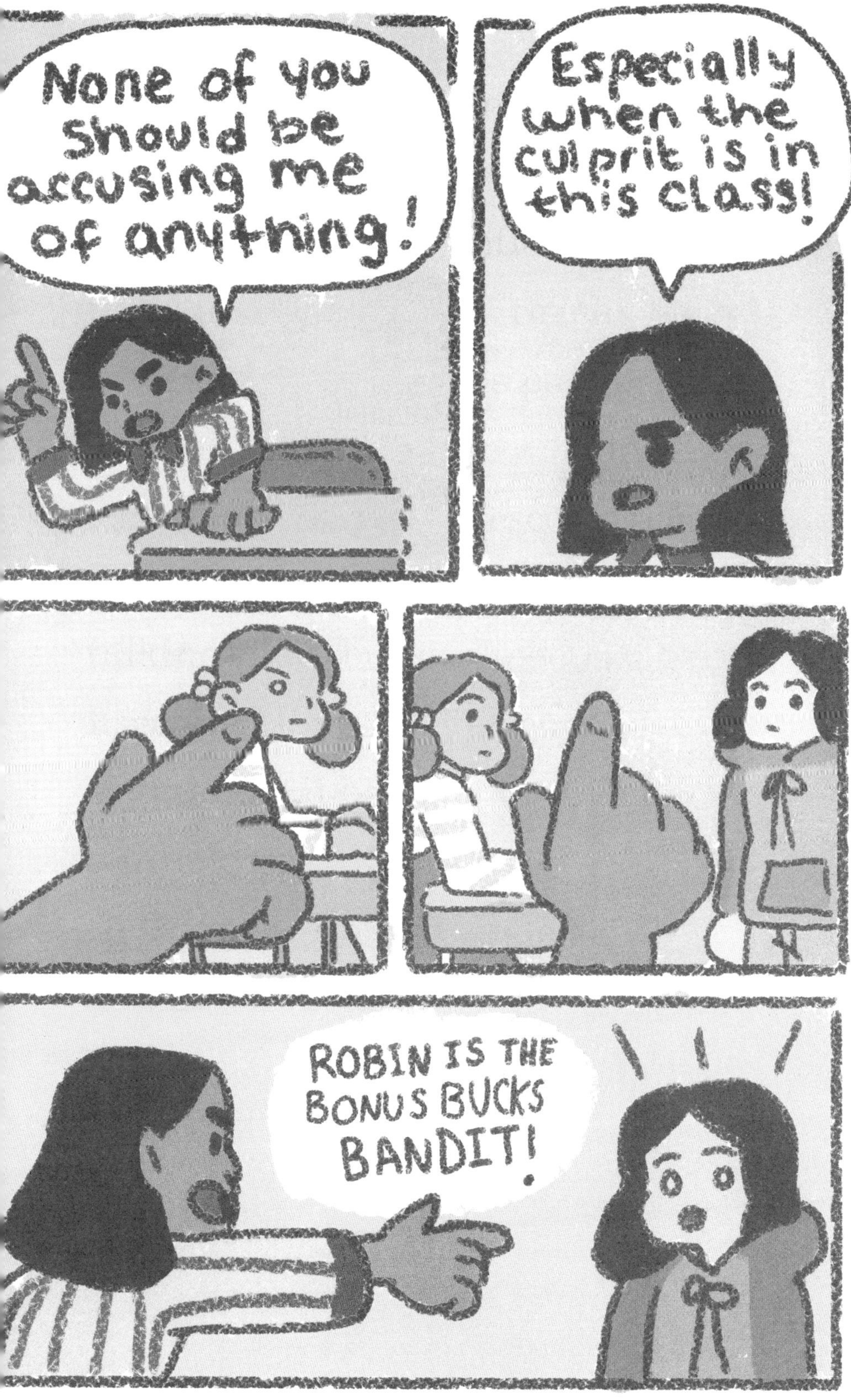
None of you should be accusing me of anything!
Especially when the culprit is in this class!
ROBIN IS THE BONUS BUCKS BANDIT!

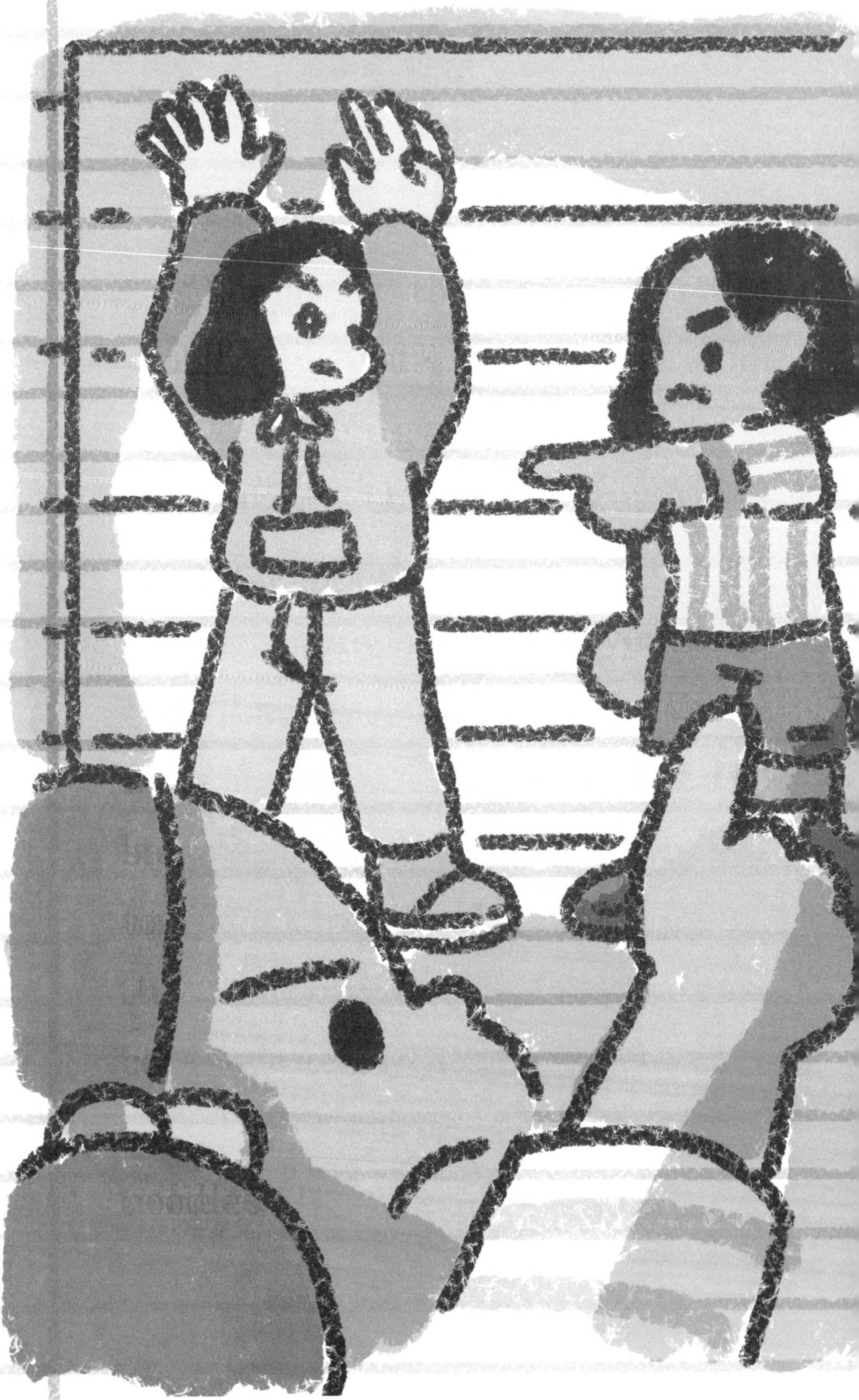

CHAPTER 9

It took me five seconds before I reacted to Wilu's pointing finger.

And that's because all the words in my head had become mush.

But then I broke down all of my thoughts and let each of them pour out, one by one.

First, it was shock. "Me? Why would you think it was me?" I asked.

"You told me yesterday that you knew it wasn't me," Wilu said. "When I asked how you could know that, you said you just knew." He put his hands up and made air quotes as he said, "just knew." "Who else would absolutely know, except the person who stole all of the bucks to begin with?"

My next emotion was outrage. "You've got to be kidding me!" I said.

Of all the people who could have come to my defense, I didn't think it would be Nadia. But she stood up next and pointed at Wilu. "Yeah, right. You're just blaming Robin so it doesn't look like it's you!"

Wilu jabbed his finger at me. "Or Robin wants to make it look like that, when really it's her!"

"How could you think it's me?" I shouted. "I'm the only one who's been nice to you all week long!"

Wilu squinted his eyes at me. "You were probably just getting close to me so you could make it seem like it was me, when really it was you all along."

LJ leaned over to me and said, "See, I told you he wasn't very nice."

I looked her in the eyes. "Nadia hadn't been very nice, but you made her your friend."

Nadia crossed her arms. "Hey! I just stood up for you. Why won't you just be my friend already?"

I threw my hood up and rose out of my seat.

And then … well, I don't really remember what all was said next.

Part of it was because I was so angry that the words just started flying out. I'd been trying to be nice to Wilu all week long, and this was how he was going to repay me? By blaming me for the missing bucks?

But I was also so mad at my friends! How could they not see that they were acting just like I had last week? If they hadn't blamed Wilu, maybe Wilu wouldn't have blamed me.

But I don't think I said anything like that. I think I yelled things like, "Why doesn't anyone listen to me?" and "I can't think with everyone yelling!"

That's the other part of why I can't remember what was said next: everyone *was* yelling. LJ and Nadia were yelling. Wilu was yelling. Heck, even the quiet kids at the front of the class were yelling.

But Ms. Gaffey wasn't having any of it.

It took a lot for Ms. Gaffey to leave the entire class behind and walk us to the principal's office. The other time I was sent there by her, she just sent me alone. And all the times she'd sent Nadia there, she went alone too.

But since she sent three of us there, I figured she didn't believe we'd actually go. Or she didn't want us walking alone, since we'd all just been fighting.

We headed to Principal Roberta's office in a single-file line, as Ms. Gaffey had instructed us.

I was at the back, so I saw Wilu and Nadia's heads bob back and forth as we walked.

I wondered what was going to happen once we got to Principal Roberta's office.

Would she sit us down and ask us who stole the bucks? What would I say if she did? I knew Nadia would blame Wilu and Wilu would blame me.

Should I blame Nadia? It was true that she'd taken bucks before.

But it was also true that everyone was saying that she'd turned over a new leaf. She kept telling me that she wanted me to accept her and what she had to say.

But I couldn't just accept what she said. She was blaming Wilu for stealing the bucks without any real evidence.

It felt as difficult as when Mom tried to give us taco pizza for dinner. Sure, it didn't look like regular pizza. It had ground beef and salsa on it. But it was still pizza. And I didn't really like it.

Was that what it was like with Nadia? Was she like taco pizza? She didn't seem like a bully anymore, but was she still, deep down, a bully at heart?

Maybe Wilu had been right, but about the wrong person. Maybe Nadia had been blaming Wilu when it was really her who had taken the bucks.

No...I couldn't blame Nadia. Then I'd be just as bad as she was. She was blaming Wilu without really knowing if he'd taken the bucks. And even if I thought she was being a bully, I still didn't know for certain that she was stealing bucks.

Then there was Wilu. I thought he was this nice kid who had a hard shell and a gooey center, like a chocolate egg with caramel filling.

Sure, his shell was more like a jawbreaker, but it made sense why. If I'd moved three times and none of my so-called friends ever kept in touch with me when I left, I'd be pretty turned off from making friends too.

But then here he was, blaming me. What reason did he have for that? He'd said all those different things in the classroom, but what was he really saying? That even after I'd tried to be his only friend, he wasn't going to let his shell crack even the tiniest bit?

So my only option was pretty obvious.

If Principal Roberta asked me who I thought was stealing the Bonus Bucks, I was going to keep with what I'd always said: I have no idea, and I'm not going to blame anyone.

But...yeah. She didn't ask us.

And Ms. Gaffey didn't give her a chance to.

As soon as we reached the main office, Ms. Gaffey marched in. When the secretary, Mr. Blanchett, tried to say something, she said, "Not now, Carl. I know she's free." And then she walked right past him and into Principal Roberta's office.

Nadia, Wilu, and I all stared at each other. We didn't know what to do, so we just stood there in the main office.

Besides, Principal Roberta and Ms. Gaffey were loud enough for us to hear, especially with the door open.

Principal Roberta said, "Cheryl, you don't need to storm in here."

"Actually, I do," Ms. Gaffey said. "I need to storm in here when my classroom is in an uproar."

Ms. Gaffey walked over to Principal Roberta's door and motioned for us to come in.

With as mad as they both

seemed, none of us wanted to go
into that room, so we all walked
like this:

But even moving slowly, we ended up in Principal Roberta's office.

"These three students are all blaming one another for stealing the bucks that have...," Ms. Gaffey paused and made air quotes as she said, "gone missing."

"Hey," Nadia said. "Nobody's accusing me! But I am accusing Wilu."

"And I'm accusing Robin!" Wilu said.

"I don't know why I got dragged into all of this!" I said.

Ms. Gaffey widened her eyes and threw her hands in the air. "Do you see?"

Principal Roberta sighed. "Yes. Well. Maybe it wasn't handled perfectly."

Ms. Gaffey crossed her arms. "That's putting it lightly."

Then Ms. Gaffey walked across the room. "I'm going back to my class to teach. You can decide what to tell them."

I took a giant gulp, like when I had swallowed a big piece of roast beef, and it was a little dry, and it was only after I'd swallowed it that I'd realized, *Uh-oh—this isn't going down easy.*

Principal Roberta motioned to chairs behind us, and we sat down.

"All right, students. I'm going to tell you who took all the bucks."

"We don't even get to defend ourselves?" Wilu asked.

"No," she said. Then she sighed again. This time, she sighed so heavily that she could have completely cooled off a piping hot hamburger all in one breath.

"Because," she said, "it was me."

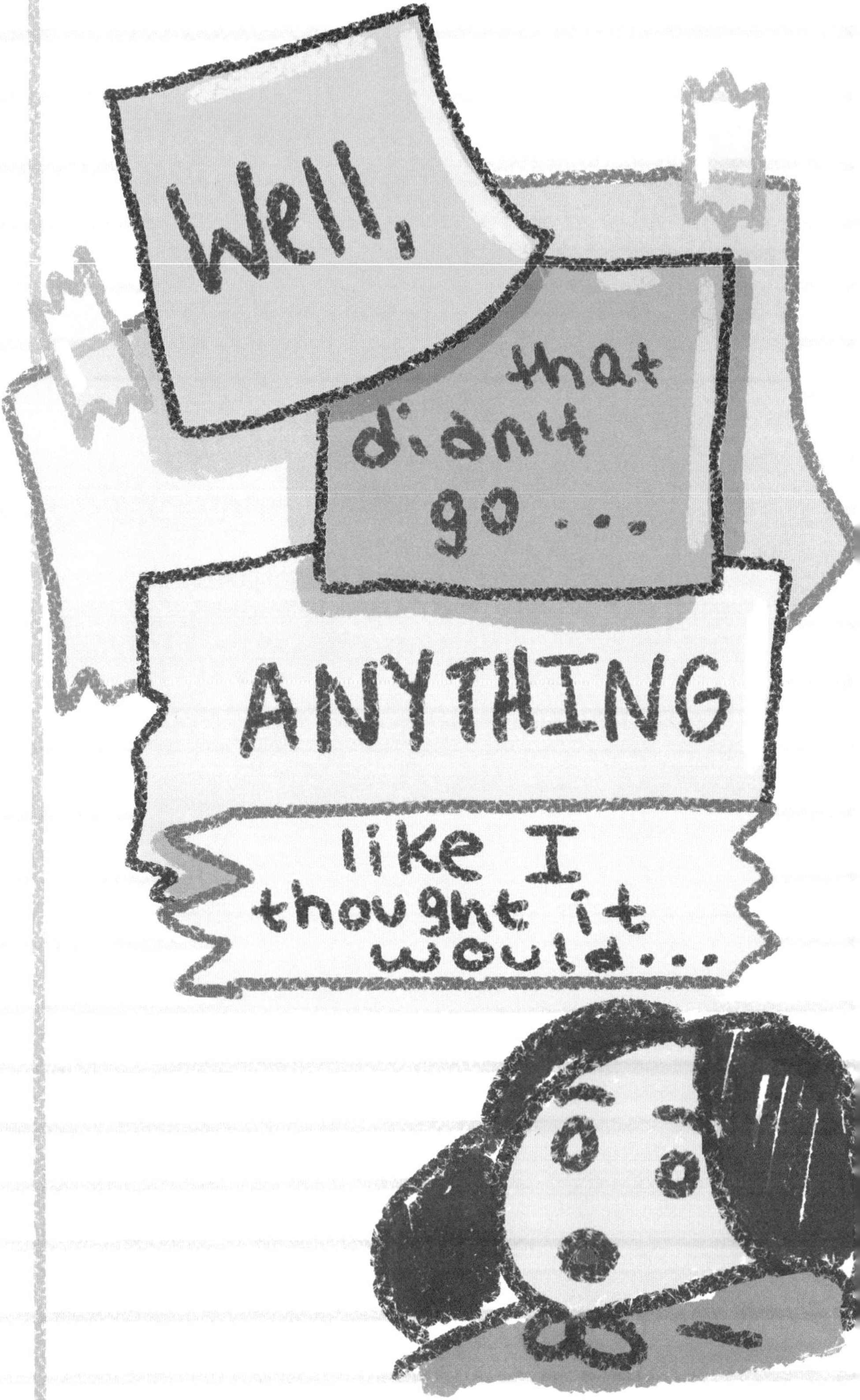
Well,
that didn't go...
ANYTHING
like I thought it would...

CHAPTER 10

The room was unbelievably quiet.

Like, I kind of thought someone could drop a single piece of dried pasta onto Principal Roberta's carpet and you'd be able to hear it.

Even though I hadn't turned my head, I was 99.99999999 percent

sure that Nadia, Wilu, and I were
all making the same face.

Nadia leaned forward. "Can you...say that again, Principal Roberta?"

"After the Bonus Bucks system was suspended by Assistant Principal Johnson, and then brought back, Mr. Johnson showed me quite a bit of evidence that a reward system like ours is not always as good an idea in elementary schools as it may seem."

"But I'm not—" Nadia started, and then she stopped herself. She sat back in her chair and took a deep breath before she said, "But there's no more taxing going on."

Principal Roberta shook her

head. "There's more to it than that, Nadia. In general, there's research that shows that these systems teach young students that they always have to be rewarded for a good deed. And then they go on to middle school expecting rewards for everything they do, when that's just not the way things work."

Principal Roberta stood up, walked around to the front of her desk, and leaned against it.

"Clearly, having the teachers pretend to lose their bucks was not the best method for ending the bucks system. And it was even more poorly timed with Wilu's arrival. That's my fault, and I take responsibility."

She crossed her arms and leaned back. "However, I would caution all of you about making such quick accusations! Especially when none of them were even close to the truth."

You're telling me! I thought.

"To that end, I'll be asking each of you to meet with the guidance counselor, who starts next week, about rumors and lies and better ways to handle those kinds of things."

I kept quiet.

I probably could have asked

Principal Roberta if I really needed to be part of those sessions. After all, I'd actually been kind of in the right this week. It wasn't anyone's fault that the bucks had gone missing.

Well, it was kind of Principal Roberta's fault. But nobody had seen that coming.

But I had been in the wrong other weeks. And it would actually be nice to talk to someone about all of this confusing stuff, like how my friends were acting so strange and how I didn't know what to think about my gut anymore.

If Principal Roberta said that

this guidance counselor would be good to talk to about rumors and lies and how to handle them, maybe I could also talk about other subjects that were complicated.

"Now, I won't ask you three to keep this quiet," Principal Roberta continued. "I suspect that even if I did, the whole school would know the truth by lunch. However, the teachers and I will all discuss how to go about changing our bucks system in a more...responsible and forthright manner. Is that understood?"

"Yes, Principal Roberta," we all said.

"All right then. You may go back to class."

In the hallway, nobody said anything for a long time.

I had a smile on my face, but it was because I was looking forward to telling all of my friends how wrong they'd been. That they'd all made this big case against a kid they didn't even know, and they couldn't have been more wrong if they'd mixed watermelon with blue cheese and tried to hand it out as pasta salad.

Then I realized that was pretty
mean of me. I didn't want to rub
it in their faces. It was important
that I be nice about it because that
was how friends should treat each
other.

Suddenly, Wilu stopped short and looked right at me.

"So...you really just wanted to be my friend?"

"Is that so hard to believe?"

"You're just going to forget about me if I leave."

"You don't know that," I said. "I'm not like everybody else."

"Yeah," Nadia said. She put her arm around my shoulder. "She's an outlaw. Haven't you heard? Oh wait. That's right. You thought she stole the bucks. So you already thought she was an outlaw."

I ducked out from under her arm. "Nadia, stop it. That's not what being an outlaw means to me. It doesn't mean breaking the law or school rules. Being an outlaw means doing what's right when nobody else is going to and not caring what other people think, because *you* know it's the right thing to do. Plus, I thought you were supposed to be nice now?"

Nadia glared at me as if I'd just told her she looked like a slice of pizza and she hated pizza as much as I did.

"So what?" she said. "I'm supposed to apologize now? Why should I? I had every reason to think it was him."

I shook my head. "Wow," was all that I could say. If after everything Principal Roberta had just said, she still couldn't see that she was in the wrong, I didn't know what was going to get her to see it.

"Whatever," Nadia said and walked off toward the classroom.

It really bummed me out to see Nadia acting like the bully she used to be. I really hope she'll be nice again. She was actually pretty fun when she wasn't putting other people down. We still have a lot of fifth grade left, so there is still time for it to happen. Maybe the new guidance counselor can help her get rid of her bully ways and keep from being a taco pizza.

Wilu looked at me like he was trying to decide if I was an onion or a tomato, and he wasn't a big fan of either.

"So, are all of your friends really as nice as you are?" he asked.

"Totally," I said. "Well, I'm not sold on Nadia being 100 percent nice, for obvious reasons. And they've all got their problems. But so do I."

"Me too," he said. "And that's why I usually get along better with the misfit kids."

I put my hand on his shoulder.

"You won't believe this, but we actually call ourselves the Merry Misfits."

Then something really awesome happened.

He laughed, loud. "You're right," he said. "I don't believe you."

"You will," I said as we headed to Ms. Gaffey's room. "Give me some time, and you will."

As soon as we stepped into the classroom, a loud tapping noise started coming from the intercom.

"Hello, Nottingham Elementary students." It was Principal Roberta. Wilu and I headed to our seats so we could pay attention.

I ignored my friends as I sat down. They were all looking at Nadia, anyway, trying to ask her what had happened.

"It has come to my attention

that students are blaming one another about the Bonus Bucks disappearing from classrooms, so this is a quick announcement that should stop these rumors from spreading.

"Let me be very clear: I am the reason there are fewer bucks. I asked your teachers to pretend they had lost bucks because I was interested in phasing out the bucks system. It was a very faulty and problematic plan, and I realize that. I apologize to all of you for being deceitful—which means I lied—and for telling your teachers to lie to you.

"I also want to apologize to the students who were accused of stealing bucks. Again, to be clear, this was entirely my idea and my fault, and I take full blame for that.

"There will be changes to the bucks system going forward, but until we have a good plan for how to make those changes, all regular amounts of bucks will resume.

"Any students who have additional questions may direct those questions to me. Thank you, and have a great day!"

The room was the quietest I'd ever heard it.

Ms. Gaffey was the first to

break the silence. "Well, I owe Principal Roberta an apology for the way I treated her in her office," she said, a little under her breath.

I felt a tap on my shoulder. Before turning around, I put my hood up. Then I looked LJ in the eyes.

"I'm really sorry, Robin," LJ said.

"Yeah," Allana said. "We were total jerks."

Dale nodded. "And we shouldn't have ever used our raps for nasty stuff. They're supposed to be for good, not evil."

"I appreciate that, guys, but I'm

not the one who deserves the apologies," I said.

Everyone turned to Wilu.

All of the apologies came pouring out. And not just from my friends.

Everyone went over to Wilu's desk to say they were sorry for thinking he was the one stealing all the bucks. I noticed that Wilu said thank you to every kid, but he gave high fives to LJ, Allana, Dale, and Sammy. I think that meant he was ready to be a Merry Misfit after all.

Nadia stayed in her seat until every single other kid had sat back down. I turned and faced Ms. Gaffey. After what Nadia had said in the hallway, I figured she wasn't going to say anything to Wilu.

But it turns out Nadia really had turned over a new leaf.

Because Nadia got up and walked over. She whispered something in Wilu's ear.

And then Wilu laughed so hard he almost fell out of his seat.

He got up and hugged Nadia.

I guess those two are kind of similar after all.

Then LJ tapped me on the shoulder and whispered, "Hey Robin, let's tell Wilu we'll all sit with him at lunch today."

I nodded my head and gave a thumbs-up. LJ told Allana, who told Dale, who told Sammy.

Everyone looked over as Sammy talked to Wilu.

Sammy turned back to us all bummed-looking.

But then he said, "Just kidding!" and gave a big thumbs-up.

It looked like the Merry Misfits would need to add another chair to our table at lunch.

Aww, man, I thought. I wanted it to be lunchtime already. Then again, I always wish it would hurry up and be lunchtime!

A TALE OF TWO ROBIN HOODS

The original Robin Hood story, which was first published in 1883, has many similarities to Robin Loxley's story.

1. Both Robins enjoy shooting: Robin Hood shoots with a bow and arrow, while Robin Loxley shoots hoops.
2. Their friends are alike too: Robin Hood travels through the

woods with his gang of merry men, including Little John, Allan-a-Dale, and Will Scarlett. Robin Loxley is one of the Merry Misfits, along with LJ (Little Joan), Allana, Dale, and Wilu.

3. The two Robins even have special friends with similar names: Robin Hood's love interest is Maid Marian, and Robin Loxley's best friend is Mary Ann.

Find out more in the original story, *The Merry Adventures of Robin Hood,* by Howard Pyle, on getepic.com.

ABOUT THE AUTHOR

Gina Loveless fell in love with kids' books when she was eight and fell back in love with them when she was twenty-eight. She earned her MFA in creative writing from California Institute of the Arts and resides in eastern Pennsylvania.

ABOUT THE ILLUSTRATOR

Andrea Bell is an illustrator and comic artist living in Chicago through the best and worst seasons. She enjoys rock climbing, making playlists, being surrounded by nature, and indulging in video games.

LOOK FOR THESE GREAT BOOKS FROM

epic!originals

VISIT THE WORLD'S LARGEST DIGITAL LIBRARY FOR KIDS AT
getepic.com